MEET THE C
MATCHMAKERS

MEGAN, a hopeless romantic, is determined to get Carolyn, their counselor, and her boyfriend Teddy back together again. After all, true love lasts forever!

ERIN isn't so sure about true love lasting forever. At eleven, she's already been in love twice!

KATIE, not the romantic type, agrees to be part of the plan, and she's the first to come up with an idea.

SARAH is busy reading *The Jealous Heart*, and she's delighted to be part of a real-life romantic drama so she can get ideas to write her own novel.

TRINA, as always, just wants everyone to be happy.

Look for More Fun and Games with
CAMP SUNNYSIDE FRIENDS
by Marilyn Kaye
from Avon Camelot

(#1) NO BOYS ALLOWED!

Coming Soon

(#3) COLOR WAR

MARILYN KAYE is the author of many popular
books for young readers, including the "Out of This
World" series and the "Sisters" books. She is an
associate professor at St. John's University and lives
in Brooklyn, New York.

Camp Sunnyside is the camp Marilyn Kaye wishes
that she had gone to every summer when she was a
kid.

CAMP SUNNYSIDE FRIENDS #2

Cabin Six Plays Cupid

Marilyn Kaye

AN AVON CAMELOT BOOK

CAMP SUNNYSIDE FRIENDS #2: CABIN SIX PLAYS CUPID is an original publication of Avon Books. This work has never before appeared in book form.

AVON BOOKS
A division of
The Hearst Corporation
105 Madison Avenue
New York, New York 10016

Copyright © 1989 by Marilyn Kaye
Published by arrangement with the author
Library of Congress Catalog Card Number: 88-92948
ISBN: 0-380-75701-X

First Avon Camelot Printing: June 1989

CAMELOT TRADEMARK REG. U.S. PAT. OFF. AND IN OTHER COUNTRIES, MARCA REGISTRADA, HECHO EN U.S.A.

Printed in the U.S.A.

OPM 10 9 8 7 6 5 4 3 2 1

For Miranda, Carl, and Emma Rehm

Cabin Six Plays Cupid

Chapter 1

Megan felt the first drop of rain as she ran toward the tennis net to meet the oncoming ball. The drop hit her right smack-dab on the tip of her nose, and it startled her so much she swung her racket out wildly. She missed the ball by a mile.

On the other side of the court, the boy tossed his racket in the air, caught it, and let out a cheer. Megan shook her head as she walked around the net and stuck out her hand for a reluctant shake.

"That was an accident, Stewart," she said sternly. "I would have hit that ball if it hadn't been for the rain."

Stewart laughed. "What rain? I think it must be raining in your head." But then he blinked as a drop hit him between the eyes. They both looked up at the darkening skies.

"Darn, it's going to pour," Megan complained. "And I wanted another game. I know I can beat you, Stewart."

"But not today," Stewart said, grinning broadly. "Besides, I have to meet the bus to get back to Eagle."

"I know. And I have to get back to the cabin. It's almost time for dinner."

Stewart swung his racket over his shoulder and started off the court. "I'll see ya Tuesday," he called over his shoulder. "And maybe if you practice really hard, you'll get closer to beating me."

Megan stuck her tongue out at him, but then she grinned and waved. Stewart was a big tease, but he was also a great tennis player, much better than any of the girls at Camp Sunnyside. Until this year, Megan had never found an opponent who was a real challenge. She was lucky that Stewart could come over three times a week from Camp Eagle, across the lake.

Tennis was one of Megan's favorite activities. The other one was daydreaming. And as she left the court and started down the road to cabin six, her imagination was in full gear. In her mind, she saw Stewart with her, playing mixed doubles at some major tournament, beating—everyone. She saw their picture on the cover of *Sports Illustrated.* And the headline on the magazine read "Partners in Tennis—and Love."

Of course, that would be years from now. After all, they were both only eleven years old.

2

But five years from now, they'd be sixteen. Stewart should be taller by then. And Megan would be ready for romance.

It was funny, she mused, how she'd never thought about romance before this summer. But ever since her bunkmate Sarah started lending her romance books to read, Megan had found them a great source of fantasies. And Stewart—even though he was awfully skinny and had that terrible crew cut—Stewart was as good a character for her fantasies as anyone she'd ever met before.

She was so caught up in this particular fantasy, she was barely aware of the fact that those few drops of rain had turned into a steady shower. A loud crack of thunder cleared her head, and she sprinted the rest of the way to the cabin.

"Megan! You're soaked!" Trina exclaimed worriedly.

Megan patted her unruly red curls. They *were* pretty wet. She went into the bathroom and grabbed a towel. As she emerged, rubbing her hair with the towel, she gazed at the familiar scene. The rain was beating on the windows, but inside cabin six there was a warm and cozy feeling. And her cabinmates were doing just what Megan expected they'd be doing.

Erin, wrapped in a fancy lace robe, stood in front of the mirror, carefully blow-drying her long fair hair. Sarah was lying on her bed, the

3

one above Megan's, with her face buried in a book. Trina was perched on the edge of her bed, listening with wide eyes as Katie described an encounter in arts and crafts.

"Justin had come over from Eagle to work on the dollhouse furniture with me. And then a bunch of infants from cabin four came in."

Megan joined them on Trina's bed. "Cabin four girls aren't exactly infants," she noted. "They're all nine years old."

Katie sniffed. "Well, they were acting like infants. They kept staring at me and Justin. And then they started giggling and whispering. Poor Justin got so red he looked like his face was on fire. I was *so* embarrassed."

"I don't get it," Trina said. "What were they giggling and whispering about?"

Katie rolled her eyes. "Us! Me and Justin! They thought he was my boyfriend!"

"That's silly," Trina commented. "You're too young to have a boyfriend."

Across the room, Erin snapped off her dryer. "That's not true. *I* have a boyfriend. Actually, I've got two now. Alan back at home and Bobby at Eagle."

Megan frowned at her. "I don't think that's very romantic, having two boyfriends." She pulled up her knees, wrapped her arms around them, and closed her eyes. "When I fall in love, it's going to be with one boy, and it's going to be for keeps. Just like Carolyn and Teddy."

4

Katie glanced at the door leading to their counselor's private room. "Where *is* Carolyn, anyway?"

"It's her day off, remember?" Trina reminded her. "I guess she went somewhere with Teddy." She looked out the window. "I hope they didn't get caught outside in the rain."

Megan smiled dreamily, envisioning their counselor and the camp handyman huddled together under a tree while the rain fell around them. It was such a lovely picture. "I wonder when they'll get married."

"I asked her," Erin informed them. "She said she doesn't know. They're not even engaged yet, just pinned."

"What does that mean, exactly—being pinned?" Trina asked.

"You know that fraternity pin she always wears? It means they're engaged to be engaged," Erin explained.

"Have you ever noticed the way they look at each other?" Megan asked. "It's so beautiful. It's true, everlasting love."

At that, Sarah closed her book, sat up, and looked down at them from her top bunk. "What about everlasting love?"

"We're talking about Carolyn and Teddy," Katie told her.

"Oh. I thought you were talking about my book." Sarah held it up so they could see the title, *Everlasting Love.*

5

"Is it any good?" Megan asked.

Sarah climbed down her ladder and tossed the book to Megan. "Yeah, it's really romantic. You can read it if you want."

Megan examined the cover. A beautiful woman with long flowing blonde hair stood under a flowering tree. Behind her, a man with black hair and a moustache approached. Megan turned the book over and read aloud from the back cover. " 'On a remote island, troubles lurk around every corner for Desmond and Clarissa. And yet, they survive, for their's is an everlasting love.' " She sighed.

"I think that sounds a little sickening," Katie said.

Megan made a face at her. "It's not sickening, it's love. True love lasts forever."

"Not necessarily," Trina said. "My mother and father were in love when they got married."

"I'm sorry, Trina!" Megan said. She'd forgotten that Trina's parents were divorced. Trina just shrugged.

"It's not your fault."

"Maybe they weren't really in love when they got married," Megan suggested. "Maybe they just *thought* they were in love."

Sarah plopped down on Trina's bed. "But how does a person know for sure? I mean, what it feels like to be really, truly in love?"

"Ask Carolyn," Trina suggested.

"You could ask me," Erin declared. "I've been in love twice."

"That's not *true* love," Megan said haughtily. "At least Carolyn's faithful to Teddy. She never even looks at another guy. Not even Darrell."

At the mention of their handsome swimming coach, the girls automatically put their hands over their hearts and swooned. They always did this when they heard Darrell's name.

"And that other handyman, Vince, is always flirting with her," Megan continued. "But Carolyn doesn't pay any attention to him at all. Not like you, Erin. You flirt with everyone."

Erin didn't seem the least bit offended by her criticism. Megan figured she probably thought it was a compliment. "That Vince is pretty cute," she said thoughtfully. "But he looks like the type who knows it. Sarah, what are you doing?"

The chubby girl was on her hands and knees, searching for something under the bunk. When she emerged, she looked upset. "Darn! I don't have anything left to read!"

"There's a trip to Pine Ridge on Wednesday," Trina told her. "You can go to the bookstore there."

"But what am I going to do till then?" Sarah wailed. "That's three days from now!"

Erin gazed at her in disgust. "Can't you go three days without reading?"

Sarah considered this. "No."

7

Megan eyed her with sympathy. Reading was for Sarah like tennis was for Megan. In fact, Megan often helped her come up with excuses to get out of camp activities, so she could read instead.

"You know, Sarah, there are other things to do at camp besides reading," Katie pointed out.

"I know that," Sarah said matter-of-factly. "I just don't like doing any of them."

"What about swimming?" Trina asked. "Isn't that boy from Camp Eagle practicing with you?"

Sarah nodded. "Patrick. Yeah, I'm still meeting him once a week. Actually, I'm starting to like swimming. Except for having to wear a bathing suit."

"Oh, Sarah," Megan said in exasperation. Her friend was so self-conscious about being a little overweight. Of course, she wasn't anywhere near as chubby as she thought she was.

"But I still like reading better," Sarah added.

"I think you've probably read every book in the world," Megan said. "Maybe you just better write your own." She picked up *Everlasting Love*. "I'll bet you could write a book like this."

"Sure she could," Erin scoffed. "How can you write a love story when you've never been in love?"

"You don't have to experience something to write about it," Megan informed her. "You can use your imagination." She looked at *Everlasting Love*. "Okay, maybe Sarah can't write about

8

romance on an island. But she could write about romance at a summer camp!"

Trina laughed. "You could call the lovers Carolyn and Teddy!"

"And you could get some ideas from them," Megan suggested. "Get Carolyn to tell you everything about her and Teddy, how they met and fell in love and all that. Then all you have to do is write it all down!"

Now even Erin was looking intrigued. "If it gets published, you could be rich and famous."

Lines of concern appeared on Trina's forehead. "I wonder how Carolyn would feel about it. I mean, she might not want everyone knowing everything about her and Teddy."

Megan brushed those objections aside. She was getting really excited. "But Sarah could make their love immortal," Megan argued. "Sarah, what do you think?"

"I think I'm hungry," Sarah replied. "Isn't it time for dinner yet?"

"Yeah, and it's stopped raining," Katie said, looking out the window. "Hey, there's Carolyn! I thought she was going to be gone all day."

Megan joined Katie at the window. The tall, fair-haired girl was hurrying toward the cabin. When she came in, she waved to the girls, but she looked distracted.

"What are you doing here?" Erin asked. "I thought this was your day off."

"It's getting cool outside, and I need a

sweater," Carolyn told them and ran into her room, leaving the door open.

Megan turned to Sarah. "C'mon, let's ask her if she'll help you write the book."

"Oh, Megan," Sarah groaned. "This is silly." But she followed Megan into Carolyn's room. Carolyn was rummaging through a dresser drawer.

"We have a favor to ask," Megan announced. Carolyn glanced up.

"What?"

"Sarah's going to write a book. A love story."

Carolyn smiled briefly at Sarah. "That's nice."

"But we don't know all that much about romance," Megan continued. "So we want to ask you some questions, like, how you met Teddy, and how you fell in love—that sort of thing."

Carolyn didn't answer. She seemed intent on finding something in the drawer. Then she pulled out a red sweater.

"Well?" Megan pressed. "Can we ask you some questions?"

"Later, okay?" Carolyn tied the sweater sleeves around her neck. "Right now I'm in a hurry. I'll see you all tonight." And she ran out of the cabin.

Sarah's brow was wrinkled. "That's funny," she said, and Megan knew what she meant. Carolyn was never too busy to talk to them, even on her days off. "Maybe Teddy's waiting for her, and she can't bear to be separated from him one minute more than necessary."

"Maybe. Hey, guess what?" Sarah reached into her pocket and pulled out a folded paper. "I got this letter today from my father. He's coming for Visitors' Day next week. And listen to this." She read from the letter. " 'I hope you're really involved with camp activities this year, and you're not hanging around the cabin reading all the time. I'm looking forward to seeing what you've accomplished when I come.' "

"Wait till he sees you swim!" Megan said. "Boy, is he going to be impressed!"

Sarah nodded happily. "I can't wait." And then she frowned. "But how is he going to see me swim? You know all the regular stuff is suspended on Visitors' Day. We probably won't even have a swimming class."

"Oh yeah, that's right." Megan thought about the past Visitors' Day at Sunnyside. The campers usually planned special programs and shows for the parents. "Well, we'll think of something."

"C'mon, you guys, we're starving!" Katie called. Sarah and Megan joined the others, and they left the cabin together.

"Did you guys notice something different about Carolyn?" Erin asked as they walked to the dining hall.

"She was in a rush," Megan said.

"No, it was something else," Erin said.

11

"Something that wasn't there. Didn't you see it?"

Katie grinned. "How could we see something that wasn't there?"

"Oh, honestly!" Erin exclaimed. "You're all so dense!"

"Erin, what are you talking about?" Trina asked.

"Teddy's fraternity pin!"

The others stopped in their tracks and stared at her. "What are you talking about?" Sarah asked. "She always wears that pin."

"I know that," Erin said. She gazed at the others smugly. "But she's not wearing it now."

Chapter 2

The dining hall was in its usual state of noisy commotion. The cabin six gang joined the line of girls waiting to collect their trays. At the end of the line, Sarah strained to look over the heads of the others to see what was on the dinner trays. She poked Megan.

"I forgot my glasses. Can you see what it is?"

Megan was only dimly aware of the question. "Huh?"

"Dinner!" Sarah said impatiently. "What is it?"

Megan glanced at a passing camper carrying a tray. "Macaroni and cheese."

"Oh, goody," Sarah said happily.

Megan nodded absent mindedly. She liked macaroni and cheese too. But right now her mind was on other things. Erin's startling observation had chased all thoughts of food out of her head.

13

"Are you sure she wasn't wearing the pin?" she asked Erin. "Maybe you just didn't see it."

Erin shook her head. "Nope. She wasn't wearing it. And you know she never takes it off."

"She must take it off at night," Katie pointed out. "She doesn't wear it on her nightgown."

"Or on her bathing suit," Trina added. "Maybe she just took it off to go swimming and forgot to put it back on."

Again, Erin shook her head. "You don't forget to put on something like that."

"What do you think this means?" Megan asked.

"Isn't it obvious?" Erin said. "I'll bet they broke up."

"Megan, you're holding up the line!" Sarah exclaimed.

Automatically, Megan reached out and took the dinner tray that was held out to her. Feeling slightly dazed, she followed the others to their usual table. "Maybe she lost it," she suggested as she sat down. "Maybe it got loose and fell off."

"I don't think so," Katie said. "She would have told us so we could help look for it."

"Better face it, Megan," Erin advised, "they broke up."

"But they can't break up!" Megan cried. "They're in love!"

Trina looked at her in alarm. "Megan, don't get so upset! There could be another explana-

14

tion. I know! Maybe the clasp broke and she's having it fixed."

Megan brightened. "I'll bet that's what happened. Besides, if they had really broken up, Carolyn wouldn't be acting so normal. I mean, she'd be crying or something."

Sarah looked up from her macaroni and cheese. "That's right. In my books, the girls are always sobbing with heartbreak. And Carolyn's eyes weren't red or anything."

Megan nodded with relief and turned her attention to the stage, where the camp director was getting ready to make her usual announcements.

"As you all know, there will be an all-camp cookout Tuesday evening," Ms. Winkle told them. "And to make it a little more special, we're inviting the boys from Camp Eagle to join us."

A cheer went up from the room, and Ms. Winkle had to wait for it to die down before she could go on. "Tonight, the pool will be open for a nighttime swim. On Wednesday, there will be a trip to Pine Ridge. And don't forget, girls—Visitors' Day is next Sunday, a week from today, so be sure to write your parents and encourage them to come. If any cabins are planning special programs to entertain our visitors, please let me know."

"I'm glad the boys are coming on Tuesday," Katie remarked. "Maybe Justin and I can get

15

into the arts and crafts cabin and work on the dollhouse furniture."

Megan started giggling, and Katie looked at her curiously.

"What's so funny?"

"I was just thinking about the way you felt when the boys from Camp Eagle first came here. You weren't so happy then."

Katie actually looked a little embarrassed. "Well, that was a long time ago," she muttered.

But it really wasn't that long ago, Megan thought. Only three weeks, in fact. On the very first day of camp, Ms. Winkle had told them about a fire at Camp Eagle, the boys' camp across the lake. And she'd announced that some of the Eagle boys would be staying here, at Sunnyside, while repairs were made at their camp.

Katie had been furious. She had thirteen-year-old twin brothers at home, and she knew what kind of trouble boys could cause. She had managed to get practically the whole camp involved in a protest to get rid of the boys. The cabin six girls had even taken a vow, swearing they'd have nothing to do with the boys.

And then the strangest thing had happened. One by one, each of the cabin six girls met a boy who was special in some way. Before long, Katie and Justin were working on dollhouse furniture in arts and crafts. Megan had discovered a super tennis player in Stewart. Patrick was helping Sarah with her swimming. But they had

16

each kept their relationships secret, so none of the others would know they were breaking their vow.

But nothing remains a secret for long at Sunnyside. And Megan remembered well the night they all realized how silly they'd been.

Erin had always been happy about having boys around. And she looked at Katie with scorn. "I can't believe you're going to waste an evening with a boy making dollhouse furniture."

"Why? What are you planning to do?" Katie asked.

All eyes turned to Erin. She picked up a celery stalk and bit it. She took her time chewing and swallowing, enjoying every second of undivided attention. She seemed to be able to tell when she was just about to lose it, too. "You know that clearing in the woods where there's the big rock by the stream? I'm going to take Bobby there."

"Ooh," Megan sighed. "That's so romantic."

But Trina was shocked. "Erin, you can't do that! It's against the rules to go into the woods without a counselor after dark."

Erin waved her objection aside. "Big deal. If no one sees us, no one will know we're breaking any rules." Then her eyes narrowed. "Unless someone decides to tell on us."

"Don't be ridiculous," Katie said briskly. "Cabin six girls never tell on each other. Now

17

listen, you guys, what are we going to do about Visitors' Day?"

"How about putting on a skit?" Megan suggested. "Sarah, I'll bet you could write one for us."

"Cabin seven's putting on a skit," Sarah said. "We don't want to copy them."

"Hey, I've got an idea," Trina said. "We could do a demonstration of how to rescue a drowning person!"

Megan's eyebrows shot up. "That's fantastic!" Darrell, the swimming coach, had been teaching them the drown-proofing and rescue techniques all summer, and this would be a chance to show off what they'd learned.

Katie shared her feelings. "It could be really dramatic, too. The person who's pretending to drown could scream and splash a lot, and then the partner could dive in and save her."

Megan turned to Sarah. "And this would be a chance to show off your swimming to your father!"

Sarah grinned happily. "I want to be a rescuer! That'll *really* impress him."

But something occurred to Megan, and her face fell. "It's not going to work," she said. "There are five of us. One of us won't have a partner."

"That can be me," Erin said promptly.

The others looked at her in surprise. Erin was

18

a good swimmer, and she usually liked showing off. "What do you mean?" Trina asked.

"My parents won't even be here to see it," Erin told them. "They're in Europe. So you four can go ahead and do it."

Megan looked at her in dismay. "But the whole cabin should be involved."

"I know!" Katie said suddenly. "Erin can be the announcer."

Erin raised her eyebrows. "The what?"

"The announcer," Katie repeated. "You'll introduce us and tell the parents in the audience what we're going to do. Otherwise, they might think we're really drowning or something."

Erin cocked her head thoughtfully. Watching her, Megan knew she was envisioning herself standing before a crowd of parents, with all eyes on her. And she wouldn't even have to get her hair wet.

"Okay," she said. "I'll do that."

"Great!" Katie exclaimed. "I'll go tell Ms. Winkle we'll be doing a drown-and-rescue exhibition."

"And we can practice later at the night swim," Megan added happily.

There was something wonderful about a night swim, Megan thought. Something that made it a lot more special than the regular swimming they did every day. It felt different. Maybe it was the combination of the cool night air with the warm water in the heated pool. Maybe it was the darkness and the reflection of the stars in the water.

Whatever the reason, the campers behaved differently when they were swimming at night. There wasn't as much splashing and yelling. About twenty girls were in the pool, swimming with slow, lazy strokes or just floating on their backs, gazing up at the stars.

The only real noise came from a few of the older girls from cabin nine. They were gathered around Darrell, at the side of the pool, as usual.

"I'm going to tell Darrell about our Visitors' Day program," Megan told the others. "Maybe he can give us some special practice time this week."

The handsome swimming coach greeted her warmly when she approached. Megan figured he was probably happy to see someone who wasn't going to flirt with him.

"Cabin six is going to do a drown-and-rescue demonstration for Visitors' Day," she told him. "Do you think maybe you could help us out with it? We're going to need to practice."

Darrell seemed pleased. "Absolutely," he said, grinning. "I just hope you're going to let all those parents know who taught you this technique."

Megan was about to assure him that he'd get lots of credit when Maura Kingsley broke into the conversation. "That's what cabin nine was going to do!" she cried in outrage.

Megan noticed that two other cabin nine girls were looking at her in surprise. Suddenly she knew Maura was lying, that cabin nine had planned nothing of the sort. Maura was just jealous that the cabin six girls were going to get special attention from Darrell.

"Did you tell Ms. Winkle you were going to do that?" she asked Maura.

The older girl glared at her. "No, I was going to tell her tomorrow."

"Well, we told her today," Megan said smugly. "So I guess you'll have to think of something else to do."

She had to admit it felt pretty good being able to say that to Maura. The thirteen-year-old cabin nine girls were generally snotty, and Maura was the worst.

"You girls let me know tomorrow when you want to practice," Darrell said.

Megan thanked him, and shot a triumphant look at Maura. Then she dived into the water, swam over to the others, and told them what Darrell said.

Sarah bobbed up and down in the water. "I can't believe I'm going to be swimming in front of people. Especially my father! Can we practice diving? I haven't done that yet."

"Sure, let's work on it now," Megan replied. Together, they swam over to one end and

21

climbed out to the ledge. Standing next to Sarah, Megan got into a diving position.

"Put your arms up and your hands together," Megan instructed her. "Now arch your back. Keep your eyes on the water. Okay, go."

Sarah went. But at the last second, she seemed to lose her nerve. Instead of a graceful dive, she did a belly flop, making a big splash in the water. When she emerged from the water sputtering, Megan smiled encouragingly.

"That wasn't bad for a first time," she started to say, but Sarah wasn't listening. She was looking at the cabin nine girls, who were laughing. Maura was practically doubled over, shrieking hysterically and pointing at Sarah.

"Check out the blimp!" she called. "Hey, Sarah, next time you try diving, don't empty the pool!"

"Don't pay any attention to her," Megan said quickly. But Sarah had turned beet red already. And then Maura sauntered over to them and spoke from the side of the pool.

"I didn't realize your demonstration was going to be a comedy routine," she said, smirking.

Without a word, Sarah made her way to the opposite edge and climbed out of the pool. Then she rapidly began walking up the path leading to the cabins.

Megan shot a look of fury at Maura and then hurried out of the pool and after Sarah.

"Sarah, Maura's a jerk! Don't let her upset you."

At first, Sarah didn't say anything. She looked like she was fighting back tears. But when she spoke, her voice was steady and determined. "Tell Erin she's going to have to do the drowning demonstration with you guys, okay? I don't want to do it."

"Now, Sarah—" Megan began, but Sarah wouldn't let her finish.

"Did you hear the way they were laughing at me? I'm not going to make a fool out of myself on Visitors' Day."

"They're just creeps," Megan pleaded. "C'mon, Sarah—"

"I don't want to talk about it anymore! I'm not going to swim, and that's final!"

Megan gave up. She'd seen that expression on her friend's face before. Sarah had made up her mind, and no one was going to change it.

"Okay," Megan sighed. "We'll think of something else for you to do, okay? Something that will really make your father proud."

Sarah nodded, but she didn't look very optimistic. And the two girls walked the rest of the way in silence. When they reached the cabin, they saw Carolyn sitting on the front steps. Megan was surprised to see her alone. Usually, Teddy was sitting there with her.

And when they got closer, she could see that the pin was still missing.

23

Carolyn waved and smiled at them. "Did you have a good swim?" she asked.

Megan glanced at Sarah. She could see from her expression that Sarah wasn't going to tell their counselor what happened. "It was okay," Megan replied for them. "Did you have a good day off?" She couldn't take her eyes off the spot on the sweater where Teddy's pin used to be.

Carolyn nodded. Sarah went on into the cabin, but Megan lingered behind. "Uh, Carolyn, can I ask you something personal?"

Carolyn raised her eyebrows. "That depends. What is it?"

"How come you're not wearing Teddy's pin?"

The counselor smiled slightly. "I should have known you girls would notice that. Well, I suppose you'll find out sooner or later. I gave Teddy his pin back."

Megan's eyes widened. "Why?"

"Because we broke up." Something in Megan's face made her stand up and put an arm around her shoulder. "Don't look so shocked! It's not the end of the world." Then she yawned. "I'm beat. I'm going to get ready for bed." And with that, she went back into the cabin.

Megan just stood there. As Carolyn's words sank in, she shivered. How could Carolyn sound so casual? How could she drop a bombshell like that and just walk away? This was a true romantic tragedy, just like in Sarah's books, and

24

Carolyn wasn't even acting the way a heartbroken woman was supposed to act.

It didn't make any sense at all. And as she climbed the steps to cabin six, Megan knew she was going to have to give this matter some serious thought.

Chapter 3

"I don't understand this," Katie said the next morning as the girls got dressed. "Why did she give Teddy his pin back?"

"Shhh, keep your voice down," Megan whispered, glancing furtively at the closed door leading to their counselor's room. Carolyn hadn't emerged yet. "She only said they broke up. She didn't say why."

"They probably just had a little fight," Erin said. "Me and Alan—my boyfriend back home—we're always breaking up and getting back together. I'll bet she's wearing that pin again by tonight."

"I don't know," Megan said doubtfully. She looked at the door again. Even though it was closed, somehow she could see Carolyn lying on the bed, her eyes wide open and filled with tears.

"How did she look when she told you?" Trina asked. "Was she very upset?"

"She looked perfectly normal to me," Sarah replied.

Megan disagreed. "She was trying very had to hide her feelings. But I could tell she was absolutely heartbroken."

"How?" Katie asked.

Megan thought very hard. "Well, I *think* she looked a little pale."

Sarah's forehead puckered. "How could you tell if she was pale? It was dark out."

"I could tell," Megan said stubbornly. The more she thought about it, the more certain she was that Carolyn's face had been white. "And I'll bet she cried herself to sleep last night. In fact, I think I heard her."

Sarah nodded slowly. "You're probably right. In all of my books, whenever the lovers break up, the girl gets very pale. And she cries herself to sleep."

"Poor Carolyn," Trina said softly.

"Speaking of books," Katie said, "I guess this means you won't be able to write your great romance story. You can't ask Carolyn about being in love *now*."

"Of course not," Sarah said. "I'd never be that cruel to her. She probably can't even bear to think about him." She shook her head regretfully. "I could never ask her about love and romance now."

"But you can still ask me," Erin pointed out. "Ask me after the cookout tomorrow night."

27

Trina eyed her worriedly. "Are you still planning to sneak off with Bobby?"

Before Erin could answer, the door to Carolyn's room opened, and their counselor emerged.

"Ready for breakfast?" she asked.

Megan studied Carolyn's face closely. Like Sarah said, she looked perfectly normal, and Megan marveled at the way some people could hide their feelings so well.

Suddenly, she wanted Carolyn to know she understood what the counselor was really feeling. "Are you sure you want to go to breakfast? We can go without you."

Carolyn stared at her curiously. "Of course I want to go to breakfast. Why wouldn't I?"

"I thought you might not feel much like eating," Megan said lamely. "And maybe you want to be alone."

Carolyn still seemed puzzled. Then she looked around the room at the other girls, all of whom were watching her closely. Her face cleared. "Oh, I get it. You know that Teddy and I broke up and you think I want to be alone with my grief."

"Don't you?" Sarah asked bluntly.

Carolyn smiled briefly. Then she sat down on Megan's bed and looked at the campers steadily. "Listen, girls, I don't want you to worry about this. These things happen. Teddy is a wonderful person, and I still like him very much, but we just decided we're not really suited for each other."

It was a nice speech, but it didn't make any sense to Megan. "But you must have loved him. You were pinned to him! That's almost like being engaged, right?"

"In a way," Carolyn admitted. "And we're very fortunate that we discovered our mistake now, before we got officially engaged and married. Just think how awful it would be if we got married, and had children, and *then* realized that we really weren't in love!"

"Pretty awful," Trina agreed.

"So I want you all to forget about this," Carolyn continued. "Like I told Megan last night, it's not the end of the world. Any time a relationship ends, it's a little sad, but you just have to go on with your life. Now I don't know about you, but I'm starving. Let's go."

As they filed silently out of the cabin, Megan tried to read the expressions on the faces of her friends. Were they thinking the same thing she was thinking—that Carolyn was putting on a great, big, brave act?

Obviously, they couldn't discuss it at breakfast, with Carolyn there. And they didn't have a chance afterwards either. Carolyn returned to the cabin with them for clean up, and then announced that she'd decided to join them for swimming.

"I need the exercise," she informed them, but Megan knew better.

"She's trying to keep busy so she won't think about Teddy," she whispered to Sarah, and Sarah agreed.

"Sarah, aren't you going to put on your suit?" Carolyn asked.

"I'm not going in the water today," Sarah replied. "I've got my period."

Megan looked at her suspiciously. She knew for a fact that Sarah had her period last week. But Carolyn—who probably had her mind on something else—just nodded.

"I still think you should come to the pool, though," the counselor said. "You might learn something just watching."

Sarah groaned, but she followed the others out.

"Sarah, you're not going to quit swimming, are you?" Megan asked as they walked to the pool. "Just because that creepy Maura made fun of you . . ."

"I just don't feel like going in today," Sarah said casually. "Actually, I'm getting kind of bored with swimming."

The others overheard this, and Katie looked at Sarah in surprise. "But you just said yesterday you liked swimming."

"That was yesterday," Sarah replied. "I've changed my mind. I don't think I'm going to be doing much swimming anymore. Erin, you can be in the Visitors' Day program, okay?"

Erin didn't seem to care one way or the other. "Okay. At least I'll get a chance to show off my new bathing suit."

"And I'll just be the announcer," Sarah said. Her tone was casual, but Megan was watching her with concern. Announcing a program wasn't going to impress Sarah's father. And Megan knew that Sarah was going to feel absolutely awful if she didn't have anything special to show her father on Visitors' Day.

At the pool, the girls paired off for some drown-proofing practice. Megan watched Erin and Trina go through the routine. Erin was the victim, but she didn't put much into her role. Instead of flailing her arms and splashing about, she just floated.

Megan, as Katie's rescuer, wasn't able to drum up much enthusiasm for her role either. She was trying to come up with an idea for Sarah, and at the same time she was worrying about Carolyn.

"That was crummy," Katie told her sternly when they reached the edge of the pool. "You were daydreaming. I had to kick just to keep us moving."

"I know," Megan admitted. "I guess I had too many other things on my mind."

"Like what?"

"Well, Sarah, for one thing. If she's not going

31

to swim, we need to get her involved in something she can show off to her father on Visitors' Day."

Katie thought about this. "I know! She can help Justin and me with the dollhouse furniture. He's coming over here this afternoon so we can work on it. We're trying to get it done by Visitors' Day so we can put the dollhouse on display for the parents before we give it to the hospital in Pine Ridge."

"That's a great idea!" Megan exclaimed. She wondered if Katie could come up with another brilliant solution for Megan's other worry. "Now, what can we do to help Carolyn?"

Katie looked at her blankly. "Help Carolyn do what?"

"Recover from her broken heart!" She looked out at the pool landing, where Carolyn was having a conversation with the swimming coach. She studied them thoughtfully. "Do you think she might fall in love with Darrell?"

Katie shook her head firmly. "Darrell is going out with the cabin two counselor. Besides, Carolyn doesn't have a broken heart. Didn't you hear what she said this morning?"

Megan was about to inform her that Carolyn was hiding her true feelings when Darrell blew his whistle, telling them it was time to swim laps. She probably wouldn't have been able to convince Katie anyway. Katie just wasn't romantic.

It's up to me to help Carolyn, Megan thought as she swam her laps. Once I've got a good idea, I'll be able to talk the others into helping out. She tried to think of other cute grown-up guys at camp. There was that other handyman, Vince, of course. But Megan wasn't crazy about him. He was the type who acted like he was mister cool, and he was snotty too. He never talked to any of the campers, only the cute counselors. As hard as she tried, she couldn't picture Carolyn falling in love with him.

It suddenly dawned on her, as she kicked off the side of the pool to start another lap, that she was alone in the pool. She stood up and saw the rest of her group on the landing, grinning at her.

"Darrell blew the whistle ages ago and you just kept on swimming," Carolyn said as she extended an arm to help Megan out.

"I guess I was daydreaming," Megan confessed with a grin.

Carolyn grinned back. "Oh, really? How unusual!"

What a fantastic actress, Megan thought as she climbed out. She could almost believe the breakup wasn't bothering Carolyn at all. It must be so hard for her, she thought, putting on such a brave performance. Surely even Katie could see how she was suffering!

On the way back to the cabin, she walked with Sarah. "Katie asked me to help her and

Justin with the dollhouse furniture," Sarah told her. "We're going to work on it after lunch."

Megan pretended she didn't know anything about this. "Fantastic! Just think how impressed your father will be when he sees this beautiful dollhouse you helped make."

Sarah wrinkled her nose. "I don't know. I've never been very good at arts and crafts."

"But you have to try," Megan urged. "Katie and Justin will help you."

"Yeah, I guess so." But Sarah didn't sound very hopeful. Megan was, though. Making dollhouse furniture wasn't athletic, you didn't have to wear a bathing suit, and nobody would be laughing at her. Maybe Sarah would discover a new talent!

Now she could put that problem out of her head, and concentrate on Carolyn. She thought about her all day. Carolyn was on her mind during lunch. She stayed there through her rest period, and all through free time. Trotting around on a horse, she felt like Carolyn was in the saddle with her.

When she met Trina and Erin at archery, she told them what she was thinking. "Listen, you guys, I think Carolyn's really unhappy."

Trina smiled kindly. "Megan, I think that's just your imagination. Carolyn said she's feeling just fine. And she certainly isn't acting like she's unhappy."

"But don't you see?" Megan persisted. "It's

all an act. She just broke up with her boyfriend. She *has* to be unhappy."

Erin spoke with authority. "When you break up with a boy, the best thing to do is find another boy immediately."

"But there isn't anyone we can get for her," Megan argued. "The only cute guys are Darrell and Vince. Darrell's already got a girlfriend, and Vince is . . . icky."

Looking past Erin, she saw Katie and Sarah coming from the arts and crafts cabin, and she waved. Katie was always good for an idea—if Megan could convince her that Carolyn was really miserable.

But as Katie and Sarah came closer, Megan could see that something was wrong. Katie looked distinctly annoyed. Sarah looked depressed.

"Did you make any nice furniture?" Megan asked Sarah.

"Try substituting break for make," Katie suggested. Then she gave Sarah a half-hearted grin and put an arm around her shoulder. "Hey, I'm sorry, I didn't mean it. It's no big deal, really. Justin and I can fix the bed. And if you want to try again tomorrow . . ."

"That's okay," Sarah said miserably. "I guess I'm just not any good at working with my hands."

Sarah's woebegone face made Megan want to cry. She was trying to think of something com-

35

forting to say when the archery coach, Deedee, called for their attention.

"With Visitors' Day coming up, I thought some of you girls might like to do an archery exhibition. Anyone interested?"

Several girls raised their hands. Megan poked Sarah. "Hey, I'll bet you could be in the exhibition. Remember that time you got a bull's-eye?"

"That was a fluke," Sarah said. "I wasn't even aiming."

"Maybe it wasn't a fluke," Trina suggested. "Maybe you've got a natural talent."

"It wouldn't hurt to try!" Katie said.

Wearily, Sarah nodded. And she went to get a bow and some arrows.

"She's got to be good at *something*," Megan said. The cabin six girls gathered around Sarah to watch her shoot her arrows. The first one didn't even get into the air. It went straight from the bow to the ground. The second one actually made it into the air—straight up, and landing two feet from Sarah.

"Concentrate," Megan urged. "Look at the target."

Sarah did. But the arrow didn't. It went sailing off in the direction of Deedee, who jumped to keep from getting hit.

"I'm sorry," Sarah said meekly to the slightly pale counselor.

"That's okay," Deedee said in a weak voice.

"But I have to tell you, Sarah, I really don't think archery is your sport."

"Hey, look!" Erin said suddenly. "There's Teddy!"

The cute handyman was strolling across the archery range. When he saw the cabin six girls, he smiled and waved his hand in a jaunty salute.

"Well," Katie said, "he certainly doesn't look like he's got a broken heart either. He's perfectly happy."

Megan didn't reply at first. She was staring after Teddy thoughtfully.

"Megan, wake up," Erin ordered. "It's your turn to shoot."

"You go on ahead of me," Megan murmured. She needed to think. Despite what Katie had said, Megan didn't think Teddy looked perfectly happy at all. His smile, for example . . . was it her imagination, or was it not quite as big as it usually was? Actually, he looked like he was *forcing* himself to smile.

She had a sense that he was walking slower than usual, too. As if he didn't have a whole lot of energy. As if he hadn't gotten enough sleep.

And his hair looked kind of messy. People who were really, truly upset about something always forgot to do things like comb their hair. At least, that's what she'd read.

And even though he waved, he didn't stop to speak to them. Teddy always stopped when he

37

saw the cabin six girls, usually to tease them or tell them a joke.

But people with broken hearts didn't tell jokes. And suddenly, Megan knew that Teddy had to be just as miserable as Carolyn. No matter what Carolyn said, she knew that the feelings between them were still there.

Whatever broke them up was probably just some stupid little misunderstanding. They were two people in love, and they should be together. And maybe all they needed to get back together was a little help.

Chapter 4

The next morning, for the first time in her life, Megan couldn't keep her mind on her tennis game. Stewart's ball whizzed by, an easy shot, but by the time Megan saw the ball, it was too late.

"Megan!" Stewart yelled. "What's the matter with you?"

"Sorry," Megan called back and tried to concentrate on his next serve. It wasn't easy. Her thoughts kept running back to the night before.

She'd waited patiently for Carolyn to go to bed before she told the others about her idea. To her disappointment, no one had been particularly enthusiastic.

"You're nuts," Katie had stated in her typical blunt way. "They broke up because they're not in love anymore. They don't *want* to get back together."

Privately, Megan had thought Katie just

39

wasn't sensitive or mature enough to understand love, but she didn't say that. She had thought Erin, who was always in love, would have understood. But all Erin had said was, "I've got enough problems with my *own* love life. I can't worry about someone else's."

She's so selfish, Megan had thought. She had turned to Trina for support, but Trina, as usual, had been too cautious. "I don't know, Megan. It's really none of our business."

Even Sarah, who always went along with Megan, hadn't been very interested. But Megan wasn't about to give up. Somehow, she'd convince the others that Carolyn and Teddy belonged together. And another tennis ball sailed over her head.

"Megan! Wake up!"

Megan tried to shake her daydreams out of her head. "Sorry," she yelled again, but Stewart shook his head wearily and approached the net.

"It doesn't matter," he said. "I think it's going to rain anyway." The words had barely left his mouth when the first drops started to fall. The two of them ran to take shelter under a tree.

Megan eyed the suddenly dark clouds with dismay. "It better stop before tonight or we won't be able to have the cookout."

"It's just a shower," Stewart assured her. He fumbled in his pocket and pulled out a card. "I hope my postcard didn't get wet. I haven't even read it yet."

Megan glanced at the card, which showed a photograph of a sunny beach and palm trees. "Is that from your parents?"

"No, from my older brother. He was engaged to this girl, and they broke up. They were supposed to go to Hawaii for their honeymoon. He went by himself."

"That's so sad!" Megan exclaimed. "Was his heart broken?"

"I think so," Stewart admitted. "He hardly ate anything at dinner, even when it was his favorite food. He said he was trying to lose weight, but I didn't believe him. And sometimes I'd see him looking really sad, but whenever I asked him what was wrong, he'd just say he had a headache."

Megan nodded understandingly. It was just as she suspected. People with broken hearts either acted like they were just fine, like Carolyn, or they pretended something else was bothering them, like Stewart's brother. Stewart could see through his brother's act because he was a sensitive kind of person. Just like Megan.

The rain had turned into a light drizzle, but it didn't look like it was about to stop. "I guess we'll have to call the game off," Stewart said. "Want to go get some ice cream?"

"Sure." They both put their rackets into their covers and ran down the road to the camp ice cream stand. As they approached, Megan felt a little shiver of excitement. Under the awning, holding an ice cream cone, was Teddy.

"Hi!" Megan said, and Teddy smiled. Megan introduced Stewart to Teddy, and they shook hands.

"How are you doing?" Megan asked Teddy casually, but all the while studying his face.

"Fine," Teddy replied. "But I wish this rain would stop. It's giving me a headache. See you kids later." He tossed his cone into the trash and walked off.

Megan gazed after him for a moment. Then she turned back to Stewart. "Just like your brother . . ."

Stewart looked at her in confusion. "Huh?"

"Never mind," Megan said quickly. "Listen, Stewart, I don't want an ice cream cone after all. I'll see you tonight at the cookout." And she ran as fast as she could toward cabin six.

She was in luck. Carolyn wasn't there, but all her cabin mates were on the floor playing Scrabble. Erin was placing her letter blocks on the board. "I-C-K-Y. Icky."

"That's not a real word," Katie objected.

"What do you mean it's not a real word? I say it all the time! Megan, isn't 'icky' a real word?"

Megan plopped down on the floor. "Who cares? Wait till you guys hear this! I was *right*. Teddy is totally heartbroken."

"How do you know?" Erin asked.

"Because I just saw him."

Trina's eyebrows went up. "And he told you he was heartbroken?"

"Practically," Megan said. "He threw away his ice cream. And he said the rain was giving him a headache."

Everyone just stared at her, so Megan explained about Stewart's brother. "You see? It's exactly the same. It proves he's still in love with her."

"I never heard of anyone getting a headache from rain," Sarah said.

"Of course not!" Megan replied. "It was just an excuse."

Trina looked doubtful. "I still don't see what throwing away an ice cream cone has to do with having a broken heart."

Megan rolled her eyes. "Trina! It was chocolate chip! And there was a full scoop left on the cone!"

"I saw Teddy eating an ice cream once," Katie said thoughtfully. "He wolfed it down in two bites."

"Exactly!" Megan cried triumphantly. "He's not the kind of person who throws away an ice cream cone. He's miserable! Just like Carolyn! Where *is* Carolyn, anyway?"

"In her room, taking a nap," Erin replied. "She said she had a headache."

Megan nodded wisely. "You see what I mean?

43

Deep in their hearts, they're still in love with each other. And it's up to us to help them."

"What do you mean, it's up to us?" Trina asked in alarm.

"We have to find a way to bring them back together," Megan stated flatly. And before anyone could argue with her, she continued. "Look, we've got an opportunity here to do something wonderful. Just think how good we'll feel knowing we've brought true love back into their hearts!"

She scrutinized their faces for any flicker of interest. At least they didn't look bored. Katie was still skeptical, though. "And just how do you expect us to do this?"

"I don't know," Megan admitted. "I thought maybe together we could come up with some ideas."

"Hold on," Sarah said. She crawled over to her bed and began searching under it. When she came out, she was holding a book called *Second Chance at Love*. "In this one, there's this girl and she's in love with this guy who drives a taxi. They have some stupid fight and break up, but they're still in love with each other. Only they both have too much pride to be the first one to call the other."

"Do they get back together?" Trina asked.

"Yeah. One night she's out trying to get a taxi, and he picks her up. By the time she gets home, they're in love again."

44

"I don't see what that's got to do with Carolyn and Teddy," Erin said.

But Megan could see what Sarah was getting at. "It's an accidental encounter," she said. "They wouldn't see each other on purpose, but the fates just threw them together. And then they realized how much they still loved each other."

Even Katie was starting to look interested now. "So you think if Carolyn and Teddy have an accidental encounter—"

"They'll remember how much they love each other and get back together," Megan finished.

Erin twisted a blond curl around a finger. "Actually, this might be kind of fun. Better than playing Scrabble, at least."

Sarah was definitely intrigued. "I can see it now. They'll look into each others' eyes, and memories of the past will come flooding back. They won't even remember what they fought about."

"Is that what it says on your book?" Katie asked.

"No. I just made it up."

"That's really good," Megan said admiringly. "You've got talent, Sarah." And then she jumped up. "Hey, remember that romance story you were going to write? Well, you can still do it now! You can write a story about how Carolyn and Teddy got back together! Then, on Visitors' Day, we'll have a story reading and invite all the parents!"

Sarah's eyes widened. "Wow. I'll bet my father would think that was really neat."

"Wait a minute," Trina said slowly. "Don't you think it would embarrass Carolyn and Teddy?"

"Nah," Megan said. "They'll be so happy being back together they won't care. They'll probably think it's funny when they realize how we got them back together."

Trina still looked dubious, but Megan turned to the others. "Now, the first thing we have to do is figure out how we're going to arrange this accidental encounter."

The room was silent as all the girls pondered this. Megan watched Katie hopefully. She was usually the best at coming up with schemes.

And Katie didn't fail her. "Teddy's a handyman," she said. "If something was broken in this cabin, he'd come to fix it, right?"

"Right," Trina said. "But nothing's broken."

Erin had a gleam in her eye. "Then we'll just have to make something broken." She got up and looked around the room.

"Erin, what are you going to do?" Trina asked uneasily.

Erin put her hands on her hips and gazed at the windows. "What if a window wouldn't close, and the rain was coming in? We'd have to get a handyman to fix it, wouldn't we?"

"How can we make the window not close?" Megan asked.

"I know how to do that!" Katie said excitedly. "Once, my brothers were trying to keep a window from closing, and they jammed paper towels in it. But then it started raining and they couldn't get the towels out, so the window wouldn't close."

Megan and Sarah ran to the bathroom and grabbed some paper towels. They wet them in the sink, and brought them out.

"It stopped raining," Katie noted, looking out the window.

"That's a relief," Erin said. "We'll be able to have the cookout."

"Yeah, but what about the window?" Katie asked. "It's not going to seem very important if there isn't any rain coming in."

"I've got an idea," Megan declared. "You go ahead and jam the window." She went back into the bathroom and filled two cups with water. When she returned, Katie and Erin were shoving the wet paper towels into the window frame.

"This will make it look like it's been broken for a while," Megan said, pouring water on the floor.

"Are we going to get into trouble for this?" Trina asked nervously. Nobody answered her. Of course they could get into trouble for this, Megan thought to herself. But only if one of them confessed. And none of them would.

Sarah was sitting on her bed, busily writing in a notebook. "Listen to this. 'He entered the cabin, knowing he had a job to do. But he took one look at Carolyn, and all thoughts of broken windows disappeared. He thought about broken hearts instead.' "

"There!" Katie tried to push the window down. It wouldn't budge. "Now, somebody go get Teddy."

"I'll go," Trina volunteered. And she hurried out of the cabin.

"And we'll have to wake Carolyn," Megan said. "But not till he gets here. If she knows he's coming, she might stay in her room."

"But if he sees her right after she gets out of bed, she'll be all rumpled and her hair will be a mess," Erin argued. "I think we should tell her he's coming."

They debated the pros and cons of waking Carolyn, and they hadn't reached a decision when Trina returned, alone.

"No one was in the cabin," she told them. "So I left a note on the door."

"As soon as he gets here, let's all leave the cabin so they can be alone," Megan suggested.

Sarah looked disappointed. "But I want to see what they do so I can describe it in my story."

They began arguing whether or not to leave the cabin, but this debate didn't go on for long. Carolyn, looking a little rumpled in her shorts and tee shirt, came out of her room. "What's up?" she asked.

"There's something wrong with this window," Megan said. "It won't close. Look, the rain got all over the floor."

Carolyn went over to the window and gave it a sharp tug. When it didn't budge, she frowned. "How did it get stuck?"

"I don't know," the girls chorused.

"I left a note on the handyman's cabin door," Trina said.

Megan watched Carolyn's face to see her reaction. She seemed to be getting a little red. That might have come from pulling on the window, but Megan preferred to think she was blushing at the thought of Teddy coming.

Just then, she heard footsteps coming up the cabin stairs. With Carolyn's back to them, Megan frantically beckoned to the others. They all got up, prepared to leave.

But that wasn't necessary. The door opened, and Vince, the other handyman, walked in.

It was all Megan could do to keep from groaning out loud. She hadn't even thought it might be Vince who would respond to Trina's note.

Carolyn looked at him with a little annoyance. "You know, you should knock before coming into a cabin."

The dark-haired handyman shrugged. "You got a broken window?"

Carolyn indicated the stuck window, and

Vince ambled over to it. The girls gathered on Trina's bed and sat down to watch him.

Vince tugged at it for a while. Then he pulled a long thin tool out of his box and stuck it in the frame. A few seconds later, he was pulling out wadded-up paper towels.

"I wonder how those got in there?" Carolyn asked.

Trina stared at the floor. Erin gazed at the ceiling. Somehow, Sarah, Katie, and Megan all managed to look completely innocent.

"Some dumb kid probably stuck them in there," Vince stated. "They're always doing stupid stuff like that."

Megan bristled at hearing him call them dumb. The only dumb thing they did was not making sure it was Teddy who came to fix the window.

"Well, thank you," Carolyn said.

Vince grinned at her. It wasn't a nice grin though. It was the kind Erin would call "icky."

"You gonna be at the camp fire tonight?" he asked Carolyn.

"Of course," Carolyn said, not smiling at all. "I'll be there with my girls."

Vince didn't stop grinning. And, to Megan's disgust, he actually winked at Carolyn. "See ya," he said and ambled out of the cabin.

"I'm going to take a shower," Carolyn announced and went into the bathroom. As soon as the girls heard the water running, they all started talking at once.

"That Vince is creepy," Katie stated.

"No kidding," Sarah agreed. "Trina, you should have put Teddy's name on the note."

"I'm sorry," Trina murmured.

"I don't think Vince is so creepy," Erin said. "He's kind of cute."

Katie groaned. "Erin, you think every boy between the ages of nine and ninety is cute."

Megan wasn't even listening to them. Her brain was hard at work. "There's the camp fire tonight. Maybe we can fix up an accidental encounter there."

"They're bound to see each other," Katie noted. "The whole camp will be there."

"I know," Megan said. "But we have to arrange it so they can see each other alone."

"How?" Sarah asked.

"I don't know yet. But we'll think of something." Megan hopped from Trina's bed and faced them. "I think we should take a vow."

"Oh Megan, that's so babyish," Erin said, but Megan didn't pay any attention to her.

"We, the girls of cabin six, vow to bring Carolyn and Teddy back together."

The other girls raised their hands. Erin made a face, but she held hers up too. Lightly, Megan slapped each palm.

"This vow stuff is so silly," Erin complained. "What's the point?"

51

Megan looked at her seriously. "The point is, we're making a commitment! We're not going to just try to get them together again." She paused dramatically. "We're absolutely, positively going to do it!"

Chapter 5

The buses from Camp Eagle were just pulling in as the girls gathered on the picnic grounds for the cookout. The grills were shooting flames in preparation for the hot dogs and hamburgers that would soon be sizzling over the hot coals. At two long tables, counselors were arranging huge bowls of potato salad and cole slaw. The sun was still high in the sky, but at dusk the lanterns hanging from the trees would start glowing. Then the picnic grounds would look really romantic.

But right now, it looked more like a kindergarten playground. The little kids were running around wildly, playing tag. Several games of Frisbee were going on, and Megan ducked to avoid a flying disc.

"How does my hair look?" Erin asked her.

Megan examined the streaked waves bobbing around Erin's shoulders. "Like it always does."

Erin made a face, but she wasn't even looking at Megan. Her eyes were on the boys getting off the Camp Eagle buses. "Ooh, there's Bobby." But she didn't make a move toward him. Instead, she turned away from the buses and pretended to watch the Frisbee game with great concentration. "I don't want him to think I'm waiting for him. Boys like you better when they think you don't care about them."

That didn't make any sense at all to Megan, but she figured that Erin, with all her experience, knew more about romance than she did. "Are you still planning on sneaking off into the woods with him?" she asked her.

Erin tossed her head so her curls bounced. "Mmm."

"Erin, I don't think you should," Trina said seriously. "You could get into real trouble."

"Don't be silly," Erin replied. "We'll wait until it gets dark and everyone's around the camp fire. No one will even know we're gone."

Katie eyed her with interest. "Exactly what are you and Bobby going to do in the woods?"

Megan was curious too. And for a second, she could have sworn Erin looked uncertain. But then she tossed her head again, and gave the others her famous I'm-so-mature look. "I *think* I'm going to let him kiss me."

This astonishing announcement caused the others to gasp in unison. Sarah looked positively stunned and shocked. "On—on the lips?"

54

Erin gazed at her condescendingly. "Of course on the lips, stupid."

Megan didn't think it was a stupid question. From the looks the other girls gave each other, it was very clear that not one of them had ever kissed a boy on the lips before. They all fell silent as they contemplated this experience.

Sarah broke the silence. "Can we watch?"

Erin was horrified. "You mean, hide in the bushes and spy on us?"

"Yeah. I'm supposed to be writing this romantic story, remember? It would be helpful for me to actually see how it's done."

"Are you nuts?" Erin exclaimed. "Kissing is very private. Bobby and I have to be alone."

Katie was eyeing her skeptically. "I don't believe you. That's not why you don't want us watching. You're not really going to kiss him."

Erin's eyes flashed. "Yes I am!"

"Then prove it," Katie said.

"How am I going to prove it?"

"You have to have a witness," Katie replied. "One of us has to watch. I'll do it."

Erin shook her head firmly. "No way. You'll start giggling." She scrutinized the group, as if she were trying to determine who was the most qualified. "Trina can watch," she said finally.

"No thanks," Trina said quickly. "I don't want to get into trouble."

"Let me," Sarah pleaded. "I'm the one writing the story. I need to see a real romantic kiss."

Erin considered this. "You promise you won't giggle or make any noise?"

"I promise!"

"Okay," Erin relented. "Maybe it will be good for you to see how mature girls behave with boys." With that, she gave her head one more toss and walked off in the direction of the boys.

"Boy, she's really getting on my nerves lately," Katie remarked. "It would serve her right if she did get in trouble for sneaking into the woods."

"Katie!" Megan was positively shocked. "Cabin six girls never tell on each other!"

"Erin's always been a show-off," Trina said. "It's just the way she is."

"I know," Katie replied. "And I wouldn't tell on her. But even so—"

"Look," Trina said suddenly. "There's Teddy."

The handyman was lugging a big hamper filled with ice and sodas toward the food table.

"And Carolyn's over there!" Sarah said excitedly. "Maybe they'll have their accidental encounter!"

"It's no good," Megan noted sadly. "There are too many other people around. Like Erin said, if it's going to be romantic, they need to have their encounter alone."

"Hey, there's Justin," Katie said. "I'm going to ask him if he wants to eat with us." Trina spotted someone she knew too, and they took off.

"Let's get a soda," Megan said to Sarah, and they headed toward the table. They were almost there when Sarah grabbed Megan's arm. "Can we go to the other table?"

Megan saw the reason for Sarah's reluctance. Maura and a bunch of other cabin nine girls were hanging out by the sodas.

"Okay," Megan said, but it was too late. Maura had spotted them, and she ambled over.

"I haven't seen you in the pool lately, Sarah," she said, smirking. "I thought you were really into swimming. And diving, particularly."

"C'mon, Sarah," Megan muttered, but Maura's next words stopped her.

"How's your counselor doing these days?"

"What do you mean?" Megan asked.

Maura casually examined her bright red fingernails. "Well, I heard she and Teddy broke up. I thought you might like to know he's been hanging around cabin nine a lot. And Joan's real happy about it." With that, she turned and sauntered back to join her friends.

"Oh, no," Sarah breathed. "Teddy's hanging out with Joan! Do you think she's his new girlfriend?"

Megan considered the cabin nine counselor. "She's awfully cute. Oh, Sarah, we can't let Carolyn hear about this. She'll be positively destroyed! She'll never want to see him again."

Sarah nodded. "And I'll bet that's why Maura told us. She *wants* Carolyn to know."

Megan glanced back at the cabin nine group. "And Maura's got the biggest mouth at Sunnyside. Sarah, we've got to work fast if we're going to get them back together."

"Maybe we can get them into an accidental encounter tonight," Sarah said.

Megan nodded, but she looked around worriedly. "If only we could find some way to get them together away from the crowd."

Suddenly, Sarah looked distinctly uncomfortable. Megan saw a boy coming toward them who looked familiar. Then she remembered where she'd seen him before. He was the boy who had been helping Sarah learn to swim.

"How come you weren't at the pool yesterday?" he asked Sarah. "I thought we were supposed to meet."

Sarah was studying the ground. "Um, I forgot. I guess I'm just not into swimming anymore. Sorry."

"But you were getting really good!"

Sarah just shrugged and looked away. Patrick just stared at her in bewilderment. Then *he* shrugged and strolled away.

"Sarah, aren't you ever going to swim again?" Megan asked. "Just because that creepy Maura laughed at you—"

Sarah interrupted her. "If Maura was laughing, everyone was probably laughing. Even if they didn't show it, everyone was probably laughing inside. Even Patrick. Look, I don't want to talk about this anymore, okay?" She turned away from Megan and headed toward the other food table.

"Hey, Megan!" Megan turned and spotted Stewart waving to her. She walked over to him.

"How about a game tomorrow?" Stewart asked. "Or are you still in a fog?"

"Sure," Megan said vaguely. "No, wait. We're going to Pine Ridge tomorrow. Stewart, do you ever think about trying to get your brother and his girlfriend back together?"

"Nah," Stewart said. "It's none of my business. Anyway, I think he's already met another girl."

"You're kidding!"

"My parents called today. They said they got a letter from my brother, and he met some girl in Hawaii. How about Thursday?"

"Huh?"

"For tennis. Thursday, okay?"

"Yeah, sure." But Megan wasn't even sure what he said. She was thinking about Stewart's brother. Boys were so fickle! How could his brother fall in love again so fast?

Now she was even more determined to make sure Teddy and Carolyn had their encounter as fast as possible. She tried to think of an idea but nothing came to her. For once, her imagination was failing her.

She went through the motions of getting her hot dog at the grill, collecting her soda and potato salad, and joining the others at a table. Justin and a couple of other boys ate with them, and there was a lot of talking and laughing going on. But Megan's mind was far away. She ate her food with the others, but she wasn't even aware of what she was eating.

The sun set, the lanterns were turned on, and in the center of the campgrounds some counselors were building a camp fire. There was music, too. Someone had brought a portable cassette player, and kids were dancing.

Sarah whispered something to Megan.

"Huh?"

"Erin's dancing with Bobby. I'll bet they're getting ready to sneak off. I guess I better keep my eyes on them so I can follow them." But she didn't seem particularly thrilled by the idea.

"What's the matter?" Megan asked.

Sarah's expression was a little abashed. "I've never been in the woods at night. It looks spooky."

Megan looked in the direction of the woods. Sarah was right. "Want me to go with you?"

Sarah nodded eagerly. "Do you know where Erin and Bobby are going?"

"Yeah, to the clearing by the stream. It's really romantic. I guess it's a good place to kiss." And suddenly, an idea came to her. Her eyes widened. "Sarah! It's perfect!"

"What are you talking about?" Sarah asked.

Megan frantically beckoned to Katie and Trina. When they gathered around her, she told them her plan. "Trina, when Erin and Bobby go off to the woods, you tell Carolyn. Katie, you tell Teddy."

Katie stared at her, aghast. "You want me to tell on a cabin six girl?"

"We have to!" Megan said. "It's the perfect accidental encounter. They'll meet in the most romantic place at Sunnyside. Erin will only get a few demerits, and she doesn't have any demerits at all yet. I mean, they won't send her home or anything. And remember, it's for a good cause. She wouldn't mind making a little sacrifice for the benefit of true love!"

Actually, she wasn't so sure about that. In fact, she knew Erin would be furious. "But tell Carolyn not to let Erin know who told on her," she added quickly.

Sarah had whipped a notebook out of her pocket and was writing frantically. "Listen to this," she whispered to the others. " 'Carolyn made her way silently through the trees. In the romantic clearing by the stream, she saw the two campers. She was about to speak, when she saw Teddy. They looked into each others' eyes, and all thoughts of the two campers disappeared.' "

"Exactly!" Megan cried. "It's ideal!"

Trina still didn't look very happy with the

61

idea, but Katie was nodding. And Megan knew Katie could talk Trina into anything.

Sarah clutched Megan's arm. "They're going!"

Megan turned to look. Sure enough, Erin and Bobby were walking toward the woods, Erin looking back over her shoulder every few seconds.

"Okay, you guys know what you have to do," Megan announced. "Let's go!"

She and Sarah headed toward the woods. Kids were beginning to clear off the tables and gather around the camp fire. It was a good time to sneak off without being noticed.

By now, Erin and Bobby had disappeared into the woods. Sarah held Megan's hand as they crept silently down one of the paths leading to the clearing by the stream. Luckily, there was a full moon that night, and they could watch where they were going. Soon, they could see the clearing ahead of them behind some short bushy trees.

Megan put a finger to her lips, and then pointed to the bushy clump. On tiptoes, they made their way there, and crouched down. Through the leaves, they had a clear view of Erin and Bobby sitting on a big rock.

It was a beautiful setting, perfect for an accidental encounter. There were lots of stars that night, and the moon made the stream look sparkly. Very faintly, they could hear singing from the camp fire.

Erin and Bobby weren't kissing yet. They seemed to be talking—at least, Megan could see Erin's lips moving, but she couldn't hear what they were saying. Sarah looked at Megan and crossed her fingers. Megan did the same. With any luck, Carolyn and Teddy would simply scold the two campers and send them back. And then they'd have this romantic spot all to themselves for their great reconciliation. Megan shivered with happy anticipation.

Just then, Sarah covered her mouth with one hand and grabbed Megan's arms with the other. Carolyn was coming down the path. She didn't see Megan or Sarah. Her eyes were firmly fixed on the clearing. And she made no attempt to avoid any noise.

"Erin! What are you doing here?"

Erin and Bobby jumped off the rock. Megan could see Erin's face going bright red. "Uh, we just wanted to talk . . ."

"You know it's totally against the rules to go into the woods after dark without a counselor!"

Now it was Megan's turn to grab Sarah's arm. From another path, Teddy emerged into the clearing. "Hey, you kids aren't supposed to be here! Back to the camp fire, both of you."

Carolyn put a hand on Erin's shoulder and they headed back up the path. Bobby walked with Teddy in the same direction, behind them.

Megan was floored. The two counselors hadn't said a word to each other. They'd barely even looked at each other.

Megan waited until they were out of earshot. "Darn!" she wailed. "It didn't work! I can't believe it!"

"Another failure," Sarah groaned. "This is getting ridiculous."

The two girls rose and started up the path back to the picnic grounds. "Sarah, in any of your books, do the boy and the girl ever stay broken up forever?"

"Never," Sarah stated firmly. "They always get back together in the end. True love finds a way."

"That's what I thought," Megan said. Then she let out a deep, heartfelt sigh. "I just hope true love finds a way before we run out of ideas."

Chapter 6

It wasn't easy for the girls to look Erin in the eye that night in their cabin. Megan knew they were all feeling a little guilty about their part in the escapade. And on top of that, except for Sarah, who Erin knew was going to be watching, they all had to pretend they knew nothing about it. Erin would be absolutely furious if she knew what they had done.

But at that moment, Erin was enjoying herself. The other girls were already in bed, but she sat on the edge of hers. She was the center of attention as she told her story, and she didn't seem to notice that the girls were staring at the floor, the ceiling, out the window—everywhere except directly at Erin.

"Bobby was telling me I was the most beautiful girl he had ever seen," Erin reported. "And he said he was absolutely crazy about me."

Megan wondered about that. From where she

had been sitting behind the bushes, it looked to her like Erin was doing all the talking.

"I knew he was just about to kiss me," Erin continued. "He kept moving closer and closer. Then he put his arm around me, so I closed my eyes."

"How come?" Katie asked.

"Because you always close your eyes when you kiss," Erin explained. "Haven't you ever seen any movies? Anyway, just as we were about to kiss, guess what happened?"

Erin paused dramatically. Somehow, Megan managed to keep her mouth shut.

"Carolyn showed up!"

Everyone gasped loudly.

"And then Teddy showed up too!"

"You're kidding!" Katie exclaimed. Megan looked at her admiringly. Katie actually sounded completely surprised.

"No, I'm *not* kidding. And I've never been so completely humiliated in my life. I don't know *how* they found out about us."

Quickly, Megan dreamed up a possible explanation. "Maybe Carolyn was counting heads and realized you were gone."

"Or maybe Teddy saw you guys sneaking away from the picnic grounds," Sarah offered.

"I guess that's possible," Erin said. "But how did they know where we were?"

Megan hoped Erin couldn't see Trina's face turning red. Luckily, Katie distracted her.

66

"What did they say when they saw you?" she asked.

"They just told us we weren't supposed to be there and to get back to the camp fire, that's all."

"And they didn't say anything to each other," Megan murmured sadly.

Erin looked at her sharply. "How do you know?"

Megan gulped. "Uh . . . Sarah told me! Remember, you said she could spy on you guys."

"Oh, right." Then she shot a steely look at Sarah. "I'll bet that's how Carolyn found out about us. She probably followed you."

Sarah managed a thin, apologetic smile. "Probably. I was never very good at sneaking around."

"Are you going to be in a lot of trouble?" Trina asked anxiously.

"I don't *think* so," Erin replied. "I asked Carolyn if she was going to tell Ms. Winkle on me, and she said no, not this time. But I better not pull something like that again, or she would."

"That's nice of her," Sarah said.

"Yeah," Erin agreed. "I guess Carolyn's okay. I could have ended up with a bunch of demerits." She climbed into bed and pulled up the covers. "There's a trip to Pine Ridge tomorrow, isn't there?" she asked sleepily. "I think maybe I should get Carolyn a present."

"To cheer her up?" Trina asked.

"No, just to get back on her good side," Erin said. She leaned over and turned out the light by her bed.

Megan lay there in the darkness, her eyes open. Something Erin had just said struck her. A present for Carolyn . . . it was just a germ of an idea. Maybe if she thought about it—but her eyelids were just too heavy for serious daydreams.

Along the little main street of Pine Ridge, girls in Sunnyside tee shirts drifted in and out of stores. The cabin six girls ambled along slowly, pausing to peer into the windows of gift shops and boutiques.

"How come Sarah didn't come with us?" Trina asked Megan. "I thought she wanted to get some new books."

"She said she's got cramps and she didn't feel like coming," Megan replied.

"Didn't she just get her period Monday?" Katie asked suspiciously.

Megan sighed. "She just said that to get out of swimming. I guess it's for real this time." But she wondered about that. It seemed like Sarah always had her period. "Anyway, I told her we'd get her some books."

They proceeded down the street toward the bookstore. Trina paused in front of a flower shop with bouquets and arrangements in the window. "Aren't those flowers pretty?"

Erin examined the window display. "Hey, maybe I should get some flowers for Carolyn."

Megan jumped. That seed of an idea she had had the night before suddenly sprouted into a real idea. And she turned to the others excitedly. "Why don't you send some flowers to her. With a note that says 'Love always, Teddy'!"

"Flowers are expensive," Trina reminded her.

"Yeah, but I'll bet Erin's got enough money for a bunch. Don't you, Erin?"

"Well, yeah," Erin said. "But I want her to know they're from me. The only reason I'm doing this is so she won't be angry with me about last night."

"Oh, Erin, she's probably forgotten about it already," Megan said. "C'mon, this is a great idea! And you'll be doing something really nice for her."

Erin didn't look convinced. And Trina had doubt written all over her face, too. "I don't think we should put Teddy's name on the note. Isn't it against the law to sign someone else's name to something?"

"I've got it!" Katie exclaimed. "Instead of putting Teddy's name on the note, we'll just sign it, 'From someone who loves you.' "

"But maybe she won't think they're from Teddy," Megan objected.

"Sure she will," Erin said suddenly. "Once, I got this valentine in the mail. Inside, all it said

69

was 'Guess who.' And I figured out right away it was from Alan."

"Who's Alan?" Katie asked.

Erin looked at her in exasperation. "My boyfriend back home! Anyway, I told him I knew it was from him. And that's how he got to be my boyfriend."

Megan clapped her hands together in glee. "You see? It's perfect. She'll just *know* they're from Teddy. After all, who else would be sending her flowers?"

"And she'll go see Teddy to thank him," Trina said slowly. "But what if Teddy tells her they're not from him?"

Megan hadn't thought of that. Lines of worry crossed her forehead. And then she brightened. "By then it won't matter. Once they see each other, and look into each other's eyes, and start talking, they'll remember how much they still love each other. And they'll get back together!"

"But this still doesn't solve my problem," Erin complained.

"What problem?" Katie asked.

"Getting back on Carolyn's good side!"

But Megan had an answer for that. "Oh yes it will! Once Carolyn and Teddy are back together, and she finds out Teddy *didn't* send the flowers, we'll tell her it was Erin's idea. She'll love you for that!"

She felt terribly noble allowing Erin to take

the credit for her own great idea. And Erin seemed to approve.

"Okay, let's do it."

The girls went into the florist and studied the various floral arrangements on display. "I like this one," Katie said, pointing to some huge purplish flowers.

"Me too," Megan said. She figured the bigger flowers the better. But Erin didn't agree.

"Those aren't romantic looking. And if I'm going to pay for them, I get to choose them."

She took ages doing it. At first she picked roses, but they turned out to be too expensive even for her. Finally, she settled on pink and white carnations.

"Could they be delivered to Camp Sunnyside this afternoon?" Megan asked the florist.

"No problem," the florist told her. He took down Carolyn's name and the message 'From someone who loves you.' "We've got a delivery truck going out in an hour or two," he told them.

"I can't wait to see Carolyn's face when she gets them!" Megan crowed as they left the shop.

"Let's go get Sarah's books now," Katie said. "Maybe by the time we get back to camp, the flowers will be there."

Megan hugged herself happily. "And Carolyn and Teddy will know true love again!"

There wasn't any sign of flowers or Carolyn when the girls returned to the cabin. Inside they found Sarah curled up on her bed, writing a letter.

"How are your cramps?" Trina asked her.

"Huh?"

"Megan said you had cramps and that's why you didn't come to town with us."

"Oh, right," Sarah said. "Um, they didn't last very long. I forgot I even had them."

Megan looked at her curiously. "Did you just take a shower?"

Sarah just stared at her. Then her hand flew up to her wet head. "Oh, yeah. I took a shower."

Megan thought that was a little peculiar. No one ever took showers in the middle of the afternoon. She went into the bathroom, and there she saw something that explained Sarah's wet hair. It was Sarah's wet bathing suit.

So that's why she didn't go to Pine Ridge, Megan realized. She wanted to go swimming. And she knew no one else would be in the pool today, except the little kids who didn't go to Pine Ridge. Poor Sarah, Megan thought. How was she ever going to convince her that only creeps like Maura would laugh at her swimming?

Back in the main room, Megan retrieved her shopping bag. "I got you two books," she told Sarah, tossing them on her bed. "Both romances."

Sarah looked them over. "Ooh, this one sounds great. Listen." She read from the cover, " 'She thought she didn't care anymore until she saw him with another woman. Then she knew the fire of love still burned within her. But was it too late for them? Had she lost him forever?' "

"What's it called?" Katie asked.

"The Jealous Heart."

Trina was looking out the window. "Hey, here comes the man with the flowers!"

"What flowers?" Sarah asked. As Erin ran out the door to collect the flowers, Megan explained what they had done in town. "Where's Carolyn?" she asked.

"At a counselors' meeting," Sarah said. "She ought to be back in just a few minutes." She grabbed her notebook, and started writing.

Erin came back in holding the flowers. "Where do you think we should put them?" she asked, peering through the leaves.

"Let's put them where she'll see them as soon as she walks in," Katie said, dragging a nightstand to the center of the cabin. Erin set the flowers down, and the girls gathered around to admire them.

"They're beautiful," Trina sighed. "If someone sent me flowers like that, I'd fall in love with him."

"If this doesn't do it for them, nothing will," Katie announced. She went to the window and peered out. "I wish she'd get back here. I can't wait to see her face."

"How does this sound?" Sarah asked. She read from her notebook. " 'Carolyn looked at the

73

flowers. Then she read the note. He still loved her. She ran out of the cabin and hurried across camp. Suddenly, there he was. She threw her arms around Teddy. "Thank you, darling, thank you," she whispered in his ear. Tears from her eyes made wet spots on his shirt.'"

"Wow!" Megan exclaimed. "That's great!"

"There's more," Sarah said. She continued. "'Teddy didn't know what she was talking about. But he didn't care. All he knew was that he had his darling back again. Nothing else mattered.'"

When she finished, there was a moment of silence as the other girls let the words sink in.

"Wow," Megan repeated. "That sounds just as good as any of those books. Just think, Sarah, when you read your story on Visitors' Day, how impressed everyone's going to be."

Katie agreed. "They'll probably think you copied it out of a real book or something."

"But don't forget to put in the part about how I really bought them," Erin warned her.

"Here she comes!" Trina called out. Then her tone changed. "But she's not alone."

The others ran to the window. "Yuck," Sarah said. "Vince is walking with her. And she doesn't look too happy about it."

"Wait 'til she sees the flowers," Megan declared. "That'll cheer her up. C'mon, you guys, we have to act like we don't know what's going on."

The girls ran to their beds and positioned themselves casually. The cabin door opened.

"It was nice talking to you," Carolyn was saying politely to Vince. Vince just stood there, holding the door open and grinning.

Carolyn smiled thinly. "Um, I'll see you around."

Vince didn't take the hint. Carolyn turned and looked at the girls, as if she was asking for help. Then she saw the flowers.

"Who got these?" she asked, walking toward them. "They're beautiful."

"They're for you," Megan said. "They were just delivered."

All eyes were on Carolyn as she gazed at the flowers with a look of puzzlement on her face. "I wonder who would be sending me flowers? It's not my birthday or anything."

Megan couldn't stand it any longer. "Read the note and find out!"

Carolyn pulled the little white envelope out of the leaves and opened it. Megan watched her expression closely.

Carolyn's brow wrinkled as she read the note. Then she frowned slightly and put the note back in the envelope.

"Who are they from?" Katie asked.

"It doesn't say," Carolyn replied shortly.

Megan and the others looked at each other in bewilderment. Carolyn didn't look at all the way they thought she would. And then Vince, who was still standing at the door and watching all this, spoke. "Hope you like them."

Carolyn whirled around and faced him. *"You* sent the flowers?"

Vince leaned against the door frame and grinned. Megan was shocked. He didn't exactly say he sent them—but he was definitely acting like he had.

And Carolyn obviously thought he had. She just stared at him for a second. The corners of her mouth went up slightly, but no one who knew her would say she was really smiling.

"Oh. Well, thanks." With that, she went back to the door. "Listen, Vince, the girls and I have to get ready for dinner. The flowers are lovely, really. I'll see you later." She closed the door firmly. Then she sank down on Trina's bed.

"Oh, dear," she said glumly.

"What's the matter?" Trina asked.

Now Carolyn's smile was a little sad. "I'm afraid Vince has a crush on me. And I'm not really interested in him that way."

Megan nodded wisely. Of course Carolyn wouldn't be interested in Vince. She was still in love with Teddy. She could never look at another man.

"I wish he hadn't sent those flowers," Carolyn went on. "Now I feel like I'm going to hurt his feelings."

What a mess, Megan thought. She couldn't believe Vince was taking credit for the flowers.

76

She exchanged looks with the others, and she knew they were all sharing her feelings. Everyone was depressed that the scheme had failed.

"Maybe Vince didn't really send them," Trina said softly.

Carolyn looked at her sharply, "But he said he did."

"Maybe he was lying, to impress you," Sarah offered.

Carolyn stood up and faced the girls. For a moment, she just studied their faces. "What's going on here?"

The girls all looked at Megan, as if they were waiting for instructions. Megan tried to sound as innocent as possible.

"Maybe someone else sent them."

The corner of Carolyn's mouth twitched, as if she was trying not to smile. "Like who, for example?"

"Oh, gee, I don't know. Like, maybe, Teddy?"

Now both sides of Carolyn's mouth were twitching. Finally, she gave up and grinned. "Teddy didn't send those flowers. You guys did."

Megan was all prepared to deny it, but Trina gave up. "How did you know?"

"Because there's no reason for Teddy to send me flowers with a note like that," Carolyn told her. "And because I had a feeling you kids didn't believe me when I told you neither of us want to get back together." She glanced at the flowers and shook her head in amusement. "It was a cute trick. But I'm afraid you've wasted your money."

"Are you angry at us?" Erin asked.

"No, I'm not angry," Carolyn said. "Actually, I have to admit it was sweet of you kids."

Erin looked relieved. "Oh good. Because I was the one who picked them out and paid for them."

Carolyn laughed. "Well, thank you, Erin. And thank you all for telling me the truth. Now I've learned a little something more about Vince." She picked up the flowers and started carrying them toward her room. But she paused at the door and turned back to the girls.

"Listen, you guys, and I'm serious. Please don't try any more stunts like this. Believe me, it won't do any good. Teddy and I have made a decision to end our relationship, and we're both satisfied with that decision. We're still friends, but that's all we are. Now, no more attempts at matchmaking, okay?" She went into her room and shut the door.

The girls were silent. Then Sarah ripped a page out of her notebook, and crumpled it. "Too bad. It would have made a good story."

"Yeah," Katie agreed. "But I guess they're really not in love anymore."

"She'll find another boyfriend," Erin assured them. "She's actually pretty cute."

"It was none of our business anyway," Trina said. "I'm glad we're not going to do any more of those silly things." She got up and looked at the day's schedule posted by the door. "There's a night swim after dinner tonight. Do you guys want to practice our routine for Visitors' Day?"

Megan was aware of the conversations going on around her, but she wasn't really listening. Dismally, she scratched at an old mosquito bite on her leg, and thought about Carolyn. And Teddy. How could she have been wrong about them?

Katie's voice broke into her thoughts. "Megan, look at your leg." Megan looked. She'd scratched the bite so much it was bleeding.

"You better get a Band-Aid from Carolyn," Katie said.

Megan obediently climbed off her bed and knocked at Carolyn's door. When Carolyn called come in, she pushed the door open. Carolyn was lying on her bed, reading.

"Have you got a Band-Aid?" Megan asked. "My mosquito bite's bleeding."

Carolyn looked at Megan's leg and shook her head reprovingly. "You've been scratching it. Go get a Band-Aid out of the top drawer."

Megan went to the bureau and opened the drawer. She saw the box of Band-Aids lying there. But she saw something else too.

It was a photograph of Teddy in a silver frame. Megan remembered seeing it on the top of Carolyn's bureau. She gazed at it thoughtfully.

"Can't you find the Band-Aids?" Carolyn asked.

Megan quickly opened the box and took one. "Thanks," she called, and hurried out of the room. Closing the door behind her, she turned to the others in triumph. "I was right," she said, in as loud a whisper as she dared.

"Right about what?" Trina asked.

"About Carolyn and Teddy," Megan replied. "Guess what I just saw in her drawer?" No one bothered to guess, so she went right on and told them. "Teddy's picture!"

"So what?" Katie asked.

"So, she's still in love with him," Megan said. "I don't care what she says. You don't keep a picture of your boyfriend if you don't love him anymore."

"That's true," Sarah noted. "In all my books, the girl tears up the picture when they break up. Or burns it, or something like that."

Katie groaned loudly. "Knock it off, you two. You heard what Carolyn said!"

"She's probably keeping it because they're still friends, just like she said," Trina remarked.

"I plan to keep pictures of all my boyfriends," Erin told them. "Sort of like a collection."

Megan couldn't believe it. No one was taking this seriously! Grimly, she climbed the ladder up to Sarah's bed.

"I still think Carolyn's hiding her feelings about Teddy. Don't you?"

Sarah bit her lip. "I don't know . . ."

"Sure she is!" Megan insisted. "You read all those books. You know people don't fall out of love just like that."

Sarah looked uncertain, but finally she nodded. "That's what those books say."

Megan glanced at the others. They were all talking, and no one was paying any attention to her or Sarah.

"They've given up," she whispered, "but I think you and I should stick to our vow. And besides, don't you want a story to read for Visitors' Day?"

"I guess so. I want to do *something* to impress my father."

"Okay! Then let's try again. One more time."

Sarah hesitated. Then she nodded again. "But what are we going to do?"

"I don't know. But if we put our heads together, we have to come up with something."

Sarah picked up *The Jealous Heart.* "I'm going to read this tonight while you guys are swimming. Maybe it will give me a new idea." She looked at the back of the book. " 'Pride and despair stand in their way,' " she read aloud. " 'Can true love triumph?' "

"Absolutely," Megan answered. "And we're going to prove it!"

Chapter 7

The next morning, after breakfast, the girls headed down to the lake to go canoeing. Megan and Sarah fell behind the rest of the group and spoke in whispers.

"I finished *The Jealous Heart,*" Sarah said.

Megan eyed her hopefully. "Did it give you any ideas?"

"Sort of. See, this man and woman break up, and they think they don't love each other anymore. They really do, of course. Then, she finds out he's seeing some other woman, and she gets all upset, and she knows that deep in her heart she still loves him. But she's got too much pride to tell him. Because she thinks he doesn't love her."

"So what does she do?" Megan asked.

"She goes out with this other guy, only she doesn't really like him at all. And the first guy—the one she really loves—sees them and gets jealous. And it turns out he still loves her too, and he's only seeing that other woman to make *her* jealous. The first one. Get it?"

Megan wasn't sure. It was all a little confusing. But one thing definitely made sense. "Jealousy. I think that's the key."

"Exactly," Sarah said. "So I was thinking, maybe we should tell Carolyn that Teddy's been seeing Joan. Maybe that will make her jealous enough to tell him she still loves him."

Megan thought about that. "It's possible. But we need to make Teddy jealous too."

"How? Carolyn's not seeing any other guy."

"There's Vince," Megan said. "He's always hanging around her."

"But she doesn't even *like* Vince," Sarah objected.

"I know," Megan admitted. "But Teddy doesn't know that."

Along the banks of the lake, girls were laying claim to canoes. Trina and Katie had already grabbed one, and were pushing off. Erin was waiting impatiently by a canoe. "C'mon, Megan!"

"What about Sarah?" Megan asked. This was always the problem with the canoes. Each canoe only held two people.

"I'll just stay here," Sarah said. "I brought a book."

Megan looked at her reproachfully. Sarah was always just too happy to get out of doing anything active. "Maybe we could take turns," she began and then stopped. Maura and another girl from cabin nine were coming toward them.

They ignored Megan and Sarah. "Erin, do you want to share a canoe? We've got an extra space in one."

Erin looked positively thrilled. She loved hanging out with the older girls. "Okay," she said quickly and ran down the bank.

Now Maura turned her beady eyes on Megan and Sarah. "Are you two sharing a canoe?"

Megan nodded. Maura then looked pointedly at Sarah's stomach. "Hope you don't sink."

The other cabin nine girl started giggling, Sarah turned red, and Megan was furious. She was just about to tell Maura what she thought of her, when she got an idea.

"Maura," she said casually, "is Teddy still seeing your counselor?"

"Why do you want to know?" Maura asked in a snotty voice. "Or is it *your* counselor who really wants to know?"

Megan pretended to study her fingernails. "Oh, Carolyn doesn't care about Teddy anymore. She's going with Vince now, you know."

It gave Megan a real satisfaction telling Maura something she didn't already know, and she enjoyed watching the older girl's reaction. Maura's eyebrows shot up. She and her friend exchanged looks. They were completely surprised. And definitely interested.

"Really?" Maura asked. "I haven't seen them together."

"Oh, they go out mostly at night," Megan said. "After we're supposed to be asleep."

Now Maura's friend looked practically shocked. "But that's against the rules! Counselors are supposed to be in the cabins all night, except on their nights off."

Megan shrugged, as if it was no big deal. Of course, Carolyn would never sneak out of the cabin after hours. But breaking rules would impress someone like Maura. And it would make them think there was a really heavy romance going on. "I guess Carolyn thinks it's worth breaking rules to be with Vince."

Once again, Maura and her friend looked at each other. "That's *very* interesting," Maura said. And with that, she and the other girl turned and headed back toward their canoe. But as soon as they were out of earshot, Megan could see them talking together excitedly.

Sarah looked just about as shocked as Maura's friend had. "Why did you tell them that?"

"Because Maura has the biggest mouth at Sunnyside," Megan replied. "You know she can't wait to tell Teddy about this!"

Sarah gazed at her with admiration. "You're right! Now Teddy will be wildly jealous."

"Exactly!" Megan said. "And *that's* what's going to bring them back together!"

* * *

As the tennis ball came flying over the net, Megan swung her racket and automatically hit it. Her mind wasn't on the game, though. She was too busy wondering if Teddy had heard the news yet, and what he would do when he did.

"Six-four," Stewart yelled from the other side. "Good work!"

Megan shook off her daydreams. "What did you say?"

"I said, good work, stupid," Stewart called. "You won the second game!"

Megan was flabbergasted. How could she have won the game? She'd barely paid any attention to it. And Stewart was *good.*

"Your serve," Stewart called. "C'mon, let's go!"

Megan picked up the tennis ball and looked at it for a second. She'd come close to beating Stewart before, but she'd never actually won. Maybe Stewart was off his game today. And when she concentrated, she *did* have a better backhand than he. Maybe—just maybe—she could beat him!

Resolutely, she pushed everything else out of her mind. She slammed her service across the net. Stewart neatly returned it, but then she surprised him with her drop shot.

It wasn't easy, but she gave the game all she had. She focused on the ball, and on Stewart, and somehow she managed to anticipate his shots. She tore back and forth across her side of the court. Stewart was working hard too, but that made it more exciting. Suddenly, for the first time in a long time, Megan remembered how much she loved tennis. And maybe that was why she won.

Stewart didn't seem to mind much. He jumped over the net, like she'd seen players do on television. Grabbing Megan's right hand, he pumped it vigorously.

"Congratulations!" he said. "Now you're playing like you used to!"

Megan was beside herself with joy. "I won, I won," she crowed, and then clapped her hand over her mouth. "Sorry. But I can't believe I beat you!"

"You're a good player when you concentrate," Stewart told her. "But your mind hasn't been on your game lately."

"I know," Megan agreed. "I still don't understand how I won that second game. I was really out of it."

Stewart didn't say anything. He just grinned. Megan looked at him suspiciously. "You couldn't have been playing too well."

When Stewart still didn't say anything, Megan put her hands on her hips and looked him in the eye. "Stewart, did you let me win on purpose?"

Stewart tried to look innocent, but he wasn't very good at it. "Just the second game," he admitted. "Not the third. You blew me away in that one."

"Why did you let me win the second one?"

Stewart's face was abashed. "Well, I thought you needed a little push to wake you up and get you going. It worked, didn't it?"

Megan couldn't be angry at him. "Yeah, I guess you're right." She grinned back at him. His confession didn't bring her down at all. Because now she knew that if she worked hard and didn't daydream, she *could* beat him. "Want to go get some ice cream?"

Stewart checked his watch. "Can't," he said regretfully. "I have to meet the bus. See you later." He took off, and Megan headed toward the ice cream stand.

There were a bunch of other kids at the stand. And as Megan got her cone, a girl from cabin eight came up to her. "Hey, is it true what we heard about your counselor?"

"Is what true?" Megan asked.

"Is she really sneaking around late at night with that handyman, Vince?"

Megan just grinned. The rumor was obviously getting around fast. Telling Maura anything was like broadcasting the news on television. Teddy must have heard it by now! Finally, a scheme was actually working! She couldn't wait to get back to the cabin and tell Sarah.

She was on her way there when she saw Carolyn.

"Hi! Are you going back to the cabin?" Megan asked her.

"I can't," Carolyn said. "I just got a note from Ms. Winkle. She wants to see me right away."

Megan's eyes followed the counselor curiously as she ran off. She wondered what that was all about. Carolyn's normally cheerful face had looked worried. Way, deep down, in the back of her mind, a troublesome feeling appeared. But she pushed it out of her head and quickened her step. It was probably just some dumb counselor business, that's all.

Sarah was alone in the cabin. She was sitting on her bed reading and looking like she'd been doing that all day.

"Hi! What have you been up to?"

Sarah held up her book. "Just reading. You know, these books are getting kind of dull."

Megan glanced at the cover. It was the other romance she'd brought her from Pine Ridge. "Isn't that one any good?"

Sarah made a face. "All these romances are starting to sound alike. A girl meets a boy, and they fall in love. Then they have a fight and they break up. Then they get back together and fall in love again. It's always the same thing."

"Because that's the way love is," Megan said.

Sarah put the book down. "They make love sound boring."

"Well, *this* isn't boring!" Megan announced,

89

and told her about the gossip she'd heard at the ice cream stand.

"Do you think Teddy's heard the rumor yet?" Sarah asked.

Megan's eyes sparkled. "I don't know. Let's go find out."

"How?"

"We'll ask him! Look, we can pretend something's wrong in here. Like, maybe the faucet in the bathroom is dripping. That will give us an excuse to go see him."

"It's almost rest period," Sarah pointed out. "If we're not here when Carolyn comes back, we'll be in trouble."

Megan brushed her objection aside. "Not *that* much trouble. Besides, when she realizes what we did for her, she'll forget all about it. C'mon, let's go before the others get back."

"I hope Vince isn't there," Sarah said as they walked to the cabin the two handymen shared. "I wonder if *he* heard the rumor."

Megan hadn't considered that. "That would be okay. I'll bet he's the type who wants everyone to think he's got a girlfriend." A great fantasy started developing in her head. "Maybe he's bragging about Carolyn right now, in front of Teddy. And Teddy will get so angry, he'll punch him! Then Carolyn would *know* Teddy still loves her!"

But there was no evidence of a fight going on when they reached the cabin. Teddy was alone, stretched out on the steps. His face was turned to the sun, his eyes were closed, and he looked completely relaxed. Megan's heart fell a little. Obviously, he hadn't heard the rumor yet.

"Hi, Teddy," she called as they approached. Teddy opened his eyes and grinned at the girls.

"I guess I shouldn't be very happy to see you two," he said teasingly. "I presume this visit means you've got some problem in cabin six."

"Just a leaky faucet," Megan said vaguely. "Is, uh, Vince around?"

Teddy's grin broadened. "Why? Do you think Vince is better at fixing faucets than I am?"

"Oh no, nothing like that," Sarah said hastily. "We were just curious."

Now Teddy looked curious. His eyes darted back and forth between Sarah and Megan. "What's all this interest in Vince about? You girls got a crush on him or something?"

Megan knew he was just teasing, but she shook her head vehemently. "No way! Vince gives me the creeps!"

"Me too!" Sarah added quickly. "We were hoping he *wouldn't* be here."

Teddy laughed. "I guess Vince *is* kind of a show-off. Well, no fear, he's not around. He had to go see Ms. Winkle about something."

Megan and Sarah exchanged looks. Then Megan took a deep breath. "We were wondering . . . have you heard anything about Vince . . . and Carolyn?"

91

Teddy looked puzzled. "Vince and Carolyn?" Then his expression cleared. "Oh, you mean the way he's always hanging around her and trying to get her to go out with him. Yeah, she told me about that. You don't have to worry about it. She told him she's not interested in him."

Megan was amazed by his nonchalance. And Sarah looked astonished too. "But aren't you jealous?" she blurted out.

"Jealous? Why would I be jealous?"

Megan couldn't control herself. "Because you're still in love with Carolyn!"

Teddy just stared at the two girls for a second. When he spoke, his voice was soft. "I thought Carolyn explained the situation to you girls."

"But we don't believe her," Megan stated. "We know you two are still in love."

"What makes you so certain?" Teddy asked.

"We've read lots of books about love," Sarah explained. "And in every single one of them, whenever a couple breaks up, they get back together. As long as it's true love."

"And we know you guys were in love," Megan added. "You were pinned, and that's almost like being engaged."

"We want to help you get back together," Sarah said.

Teddy smiled, but it wasn't his usual teasing grin. "I know you girls have good intentions. Carolyn told me about the flowers. And I hate to sound like a know-it-all grown-up, but you kids are young, and you really don't know anything yet about love and relationships."

"We've read lots of books," Megan insisted, but Teddy shook his head.

"Romance books aren't like real life," he said. "They're more like fantasies or fairy tales. In real life, people change, and feelings change. Carolyn and I are still friends. But we're not in love anymore."

Megan was about to argue, but something in his expression stopped her. And then, an awful realization hit her. She tried to fight it out of her head, but it was no use. Looking into Teddy's eyes, she knew he was telling the truth. Carolyn and Teddy had split up for good. And there was absolutely positively nothing they could do about it.

Sarah seemed to know this too. "Then—there's no hope?"

"It's not a tragedy!" Teddy exclaimed. "We're still friends! And Carolyn will meet someone new, and I'll meet someone new. Don't worry about us! And quit trying to get us back together!"

"Okay," Megan said. She was wondering if they should apologize for all their schemes when she heard footsteps behind her.

Vince was coming up the path. He didn't speak to the girls as he started up the steps. He just marched into the cabin, letting the door slam shut.

Teddy glanced at him over his shoulder. Then he turned back to the girls. "Now, tell me about your leaky faucet. It is actually running or just dripping?"

Before Megan or Sarah could come up with anything, the cabin door opened again. Vince came out, carrying a pile of clothes in his arms. He went to the car parked in front, tossed the clothes in, and came back.

"What's up?" Teddy asked him.

Vince's lip curled. "Looks like you'll have this cabin all to yourself, buddy. I've been fired." He went back into the cabin, letting the door slam again.

Megan stared at the closed door. For the second time that day, a strange and uncomfortable feeling hit her. This time it wasn't quite so easy to push it out of her head. She looked at Sarah. Did she look a little pale, or was that her imagination?

Teddy jumped up. "I better find out what's going on," he said to the girls. Then his face grew serious. "But about what we were talking about before—you kids have to accept the fact that we're older and we know what we're doing. To put it bluntly, what's happened between Carolyn and me is really none of your business. And if you keep interfering, you could do more

94

harm than good." Something in his tone made Megan shiver.

"Oh—and I'll come see about your faucet in a few minutes," he added.

"Don't bother," Megan said quickly. "I mean, it might not be leaking anymore. We'll let you know if it is."

Teddy grinned. Then he opened the door and disappeared inside the cabin.

The girls started walking back to their cabin. For a few moments they were silent. Then Megan spoke. "I wonder how come Vince got fired?" Even as she spoke, she could hear her voice shaking.

Sarah's voice sounded funny too. "Are you thinking what I'm thinking?"

Resolutely, Megan shook her head. "It's not possible. I mean, Maura's a big mouth, but she wouldn't go and tell Ms. Winkle, would she?"

"I doubt it," Sarah said quickly. "Besides, Ms. Winkle wouldn't listen to gossip, would she?"

"Absolutely not," Megan said. But she realized that both she and Sarah were walking more rapidly. And the closer they got to cabin six, the faster they walked.

"We better be quiet," Sarah said breathlessly, as they approached the steps. "It's still rest period."

But no one in the cabin was resting. Trina,

Katie, and Erin were huddled on Trina's bed. All three looked positively stunned.

"What's going on?" Sarah asked.

Trina looked up, and Megan realized that Trina's eyes were full of tears.

"Carolyn's leaving."

Chapter 8

Megan swallowed with difficulty. "What did you say?"

Trina wiped her eyes. "Carolyn's leaving Sunnyside. Today. She's packing her bags right now."

Megan turned and looked at the closed door leading to Carolyn's room. Then she sank to the floor next to Trina's bed. "Why?"

Katie shrugged woefully. "We don't know. She won't tell us."

"She just came back a few minutes ago," Erin explained. "She looked awful, really pale, and her eyes were red. She told us she was leaving, and we'd be getting a new counselor, and she didn't want to discuss it. Then she went into her room and started packing."

Megan glanced up at Sarah, who was still standing there as if she were frozen in position. "She didn't say why she was leaving?" she finally managed to ask. "She didn't even give you a hint?"

Trina shook her head and twisted her fingers nervously. "Do you think it was us? Something we did?"

"But we haven't done anything that awful," Erin objected. "Okay, maybe we broke a few itsy-bitsy rules. But nothing major."

"Maybe she was really mad about Erin and Bobby sneaking away from the camp fire," Katie suggested.

Erin glared at her. "Well, it was your idea to trick her with those flowers. Or maybe it was Megan's idea."

"Let's not fight," Megan pleaded. "I'm sure that's not why she's leaving."

"How do you know?" Erin asked.

Megan wasn't absolutely sure. But she was having some pretty awful suspicions.

"Where have you guys been, anyway?" Katie asked her.

"We went to see Teddy."

"Megan!" Katie shrieked. "Will you get off it! I'll bet that's why Carolyn's leaving. She's sick of you trying to get her and Teddy back together."

Sarah spoke up quickly. "It's okay, we're giving up. Hey, you know who else is leaving? Vince! He's been fired."

Erin's eyes lit up. "Maybe that's why Carolyn's leaving!"

"Are you nuts?" Katie demanded. "Why would she care if Vince was fired? She doesn't even like him."

Erin smirked. "That's what she told us. Maybe she just didn't want us to know her real feelings. Maybe she's madly in love with him, and she doesn't want to stay here if he leaves."

"That's crazy," Katie stated. "Vince is creepy."

"Opposites attract," Sarah murmured. "That happened in one of the books I read. A nice girl fell in love with a bad guy."

"But he's not Carolyn's type," Trina insisted.

"How do you know what Carolyn's type is?" Erin snapped.

Megan eyes swept the group. They were all upset and irritable, but no one was feeling worse than she was. And all this guessing was pointless. She jumped up.

"I'm going to find out what happened." She marched to Carolyn's door and knocked. "Carolyn? Can we talk to you?"

The door opened almost immediately. Carolyn looked just the way Erin described her—pale, and her eyes were still red. Her attempt at a smile wasn't very successful. "Hi, Megan. What do you want?"

"We want to know why you're leaving."

Carolyn was quiet. Then she came out of the room, and faced the group. "Girls, I really don't want to talk about this."

99

"Are you angry at us?" Trina asked. "Did we do something to make you want to leave?"

"Oh no, Trina!" Carolyn exclaimed. "It has nothing to do with you guys." She sighed, and then she put her hand to her head, as if it hurt. "I suppose I do owe you an explanation of sorts. Besides, the way rumors spread in this camp, you'll probably hear about this anyway." She paused, as if trying to find the right words. "I'm not leaving because I want to. I've been asked to leave."

Except for Trina's gasp, there was total silence as the girls absorbed this startling information. Then Katie spoke. "You mean—you were fired?"

Carolyn nodded. As she gazed at their faces, she smiled slightly. "I can see you're all shocked. Well, I'm shocked too. This is a new experience for me. I've never been fired from a job before."

Trina was totally bewildered. "But why were you fired? You're a terrific counselor."

"I'm glad you think so," Carolyn replied. "But I'm afraid Ms. Winkle doesn't share your opinion." She shook her head sadly. Her eyes strayed away from the girls, and in her next words she seemed to be talking to herself. "I still don't understand why she believed those ridiculous rumors . . ."

Megan's stomach jumped. She looked at

100

Sarah. "What—what rumors?" Sarah asked weakly.

"Oh, nothing," Carolyn said quickly. "Girls, I have to get back to packing. And you're supposed to be resting." She went back into her room and shut the door.

"I wonder what she meant?" Trina asked. "Why would anyone spread rumors about Carolyn?"

"Oh, Megan," Sarah moaned. "What are we going to do?"

Megan couldn't speak. Her insides were churning, and her mind felt like there was a tornado running through it. Somehow, though, she forced herself to think. And it wasn't long before she knew what they had to do. It might mean total disgrace and a zillion demerits. They might even get sent home. But none of that mattered. "We're going to see Ms. Winkle."

Sarah went positively green. But she put on her bravest face as she nodded. "Okay."

The others were looking at them curiously. "Why are you going to see Ms. Winkle?" Trina asked.

Megan swallowed. "So we can tell her the rumor isn't true."

"But you don't even know what the rumor is," Erin said.

"Yes, we do." Sarah's voice trembled.

And so did Megan's when she said, "I started it."

The look of horror on her cabinmates' faces was too much to bear. Megan focused on the floor as she explained. "We thought you guys were giving up on Carolyn and Teddy too easily. And we decided we could get them together if we could make Teddy jealous. So I made up this story about Carolyn sneaking out at night to see Vince. And I told Maura."

"Maura from cabin nine?" Katie asked, her tone aghast. "The biggest mouth at Sunnyside?"

Megan nodded miserably and raised her head to face them. They all looked pretty grim. Even Trina, who never got angry, was gazing at her sternly.

"That was a very stupid thing to do, Megan. Do you realize how much trouble you've caused?"

Megan could only nod again. And Sarah was sniffling. "I guess that's why Vince got fired too," she mumbled.

Megan hadn't even considered Vince. And that made her feel worse. Vince might be a creep, but he didn't deserve to be fired because of a rumor.

"It's strange, though," Katie mused. "Ms. Winkle's pretty fair. I wonder how come she believed a rumor?"

"People always believe rumors," Erin assured her. "Last year at school, we started a rumor that this girl had lice in her hair. And everyone stayed away from her for ages."

"But Ms. Winkle's not in the sixth grade," Katie pointed out.

And Trina looked at Erin disapprovingly. "Erin, that's terrible."

Erin shrugged. "She deserved it. She was a creep. She was always telling on other kids."

Katie stood up. "Well, Carolyn's not a creep, and she doesn't deserve to be fired. Are you guys going to see Ms. Winkle now?"

Megan and Sarah nodded. Katie turned to Trina and Erin. "I think we should go with them. After all, we were in on this whole silly matchmaking business too."

"I don't want to get into trouble," Erin whined, but Katie stood firm.

"Erin, cabin six girls stick together, remember?"

Erin still didn't look too thrilled with the idea, but she got up. Trina was already at the door. And nobody gave a thought to the fact that it was rest period. This was an emergency.

Nobody said much on the way to Ms. Winkle's office. Megan couldn't remember ever feeling so terrible before. Somehow she'd managed to get two people fired. Her cabinmates were furious with her. And she might even get sent home. She didn't even want to imagine what her parents would say. She'd probably be grounded for life.

"Look!" Katie said. "There's Vince." He was walking up the steps to Ms. Winkle's cabin.

"Oh, good, he hasn't left yet," Megan said. Surely, after Ms. Winkle heard her confession, he'd get his job back.

Silently, they climbed the steps to Ms. Winkle's cabin, and went into the outer office. The secretary was handing Vince an envelope.

"Here's your paycheck," she said.

Vince didn't even thank her. He stuffed it in the pocket of his jeans and turned to leave.

"Wait!" Megan said. Vince glared at her with his usual surly expression.

"What do you want?"

Megan's words came out in a rush. "We know why you were fired. And we know it's not true, the rumor about you and Carolyn. We're going to tell Ms. Winkle right now. And I'll bet she gives you your job back."

Vince sneered. "Don't bother. I don't want this lousy job back. I was planning to quit anyway."

"We're still going to tell her," Sarah said. "Carolyn got fired too!"

Vince grinned in a very unpleasant way. "Yeah, I figured she'd get fired after what I told Winkle."

"What did you tell Wink—I mean, Ms. Winkle?" Megan asked.

Vince's grin got wider and nastier. "I told her the rumors were true."

Megan was speechless, and Katie took over. "Why did you do that?"

"Because I wouldn't go out with you." The girls whirled around to see Carolyn standing in the doorway. She didn't even glance at them. "And you decided to get back at me."

"That's right," Vince began, but he was interrupted by a voice coming from a door that had just opened.

"You know, these walls are paper thin," Ms. Winkle said. Her mouth was set in a thin line. "Would you all please step into my office?"

Chapter 9

Two days later, Megan sat on a bench and scanned the road ahead for her parents' car. She was very happy knowing they were coming for Visitors' Day, and not to take her home.

All over the picnic grounds, campers were having reunions with their families. A few feet away from her, Trina's mother was talking with Sarah's father, and Erin was flirting with Katie's twin brothers. Sarah joined her at the bench.

"I can't believe we're still here. I thought for sure that Ms. Winkle was going to send us home."

"I thought so too," Megan said. "And all we got were five demerits." She grinned. "Ms. Winkle said she wasn't sure how many demerits to give us. She'd never had a case of faulty matchmaking before."

"That wasn't all we got," Sarah reminded her.

"We don't get to go to Pine Ridge for two weeks." She sighed. "I'll have to get Katie to pick up books for me. Not romances, though," she added hastily.

"At least Carolyn got her job back," Megan noted. "That's the most important thing. And I don't think she hates us for what we did."

Sarah shook her head. "I'm pretty sure she's forgiven us." She grinned. "She said she never wanted to see me reading romances again, though. That's okay with me. I was sick of them anyway."

"She asked me if I could please stop daydreaming," Megan said.

"Can you?" Sarah asked.

Megan giggled. "I don't think so. But I promised her I'd stop trying to turn my daydreams into real life!"

"I think she was a lot madder at Vince than at us," Sarah said. "She really let him have it in Ms. Winkle's office."

"Yeah. In a way, we were lucky. Ms. Winkle was so furious when she found out he lied to her, she almost forgot about us."

"Well, not exactly," Sarah murmured.

She was right. They'd all received a pretty severe lecture from the camp director. And Megan, in particular, got a stern scolding for letting her fantasies get out of hand and interfering with other people's lives.

"I'm glad it's all over." She gave Sarah a

107

sidelong glance. "It's too bad you didn't get to write your story, though."

Sarah wrinkled her nose. "I didn't really want to write it anyway. All that romantic stuff was getting boring."

"But now you don't have anything to do to impress your father," Megan pointed out. Then, suddenly, in the back of her mind, the spark of an idea appeared.

"Yeah, I know." Sarah stared straight ahead. "But I'll still introduce the swimming exhibition. That's something, I guess. Hey, Megan, aren't those your parents?"

Megan's idea had started to grow, and her thoughts were far away. But Sarah's words jerked her back to reality. She leaped up from the bench and tore across the field to greet her mother and father.

For the next few minutes, Megan was occupied with hugs and kisses and introducing her parents to Carolyn. They'd met the other cabin six girls and their parents before, so everyone was talking at once and catching up on news. Megan had a brief moment of panic when Ms. Winkle joined their group.

"I hope Megan hasn't been giving you all too much trouble this summer," Megan's mother said, smiling at Carolyn and Ms. Winkle. "She's been known to daydream her way into a lot of mischief back home."

"Oh, *really?*" Carolyn raised her eyebrows, as

if this were news to her. Megan watched anxiously as her counselor and Ms. Winkle exchanged knowing looks. "Oh, we don't mind a little daydream or two," Ms. Winkle said smoothly. "As long as that daydream stays in her head." She drifted away to greet another family, and Megan's father gave his daughter a look she knew very well.

"Megan, have you been acting out your fantasies again?"

"Who me?" Megan asked with all the innocence she could muster.

Her mother laughed and turned to Carolyn. "When I gave birth to Megan's brother three years ago, Megan became convinced I'd been given the wrong baby in the hospital. Every time she saw a baby, she'd insist he was my *real* son."

"Mom, I was only eight years old!" Megan cried. "But you have to admit, he didn't look anything like the rest of us."

"Megan's got a good imagination," Carolyn told her parents. "Maybe someday she'll put it to good use." And she winked at Megan.

Megan squirmed. Luckily, Ms. Winkle rang a bell just then, announcing it was time for lunch. Everyone headed for the grills, and for the time being, Megan's imagination was not the central topic of conversation.

They all gathered with their food at a big picnic table—the cabin six girls, Sarah's father, Trina's mother, Katie's parents and her brothers, and Megan's parents. Erin's parents couldn't come, since they were in Europe on vacation. But Erin didn't seem to mind. She looked perfectly happy having two thirteen-year-old boys to flirt with.

"We're doing an exhibition at the swimming pool after lunch," Katie announced to the parents.

"Wonderful," Sarah's father said, beaming at his daughter. "I'm happy to hear you're more involved with camp activities this summer."

Sarah produced a weak smile. Watching her, Megan recalled the little idea she'd had earlier. Slowly, it began turning into a real plan. She wasn't absolutely sure if she could pull it off, but it was definitely worth a try . . .

"Megan!"

She was suddenly aware of Katie tugging on her arm. She put her daydreams on hold. "What?"

"C'mon, we have to get ready!"

Megan hopped up. "See you at the pool!" she called to her parents, and took off with the others.

Back in cabin six, the girls quickly put on their bathing suits. Only Sarah remained in her shorts and tee shirt.

"Sarah, I think you should put on a suit too," Megan suggested.

"Why? I'm not going in the water. I'm just introducing everyone."

Megan thought rapidly. "Well, it would *look* better, if we're all dressed alike. That way they'll see we're all cabin six girls and part of the same team."

Sarah's forehead wrinkled. "Megan, it's just our parents! They *know* who we are."

"It'll look better," Megan insisted.

Sarah still seemed skeptical. But she was used to Megan's crazy notions, so finally she shrugged and said, "Okay." And she put on her suit.

"Now, we have to make this look good," Megan reminded them as they walked to the pool. "Erin, you and Katie have to splash around a lot and yell and try to look like you're really drowning, okay? Then, on the count of three, Trina and I will dive and do the rescue."

"Just try not to choke me when you grab me around the neck, okay?" Katie asked Megan. "Remember, you're supposed to be saving me, not strangling me."

"Okay," Megan said, not really listening. "Hey, anyone want to race me to the pool?" Without waiting for an answer, she sprinted on ahead. She knew no one would take her up on her offer. And she needed to get to the pool first. There was something she had to tell Darrell.

All the families, plus Carolyn, were sitting on the benches alongside the pool. Megan waved to

111

them, and then ran over to the swimming coach. She had to tell him her plan so he wouldn't interfere.

She'd worried a little that Darrell would disapprove, but he actually seemed amused by the idea. And he promised he wouldn't do anything to mess it up.

The girls gathered at the edge of the pool. Sarah faced the audience.

"Ladies and gentlemen, cabin six welcomes you to Camp Sunnyside. We have planned this exhibition to show you something very important that we've learned here. Here at Sunnyside, we spend a lot of time in the pool, and our swimming coach, Darrell, gives us lessons every day."

At the mention of Darrell, Megan automatically put her hand over her heart. Only a nudge from Katie kept her from going into their usual swoon.

"But sometimes, even good swimmers can get into trouble in the water," Sarah continued. "So we also learn how to save each other. I now present Katie, Erin, Megan, and Trina, who will show you how a friend in need is a friend indeed!"

Katie and Erin jumped into the water and swam to the center. Katie started waving her arms wildly and making weird faces. Then she started yelling, "I'm drowning! Save me! I'm going under!"

Erin wasn't quite as dramatic. She floated on her stomach, face down, and raised her head every few seconds to croak, "Help, help."

Megan and Trina were poised at the pool's edge. "One, two, three," Megan counted, and they dove into the water. Megan swam to Katie, Trina swam to Erin, and they immediately grasped their victims in the proper rescue hold.

Megan could hear Erin wailing, "Don't rip my suit straps!" Of course, Erin was the type who would worry about how she looked when she was drowning.

Megan was having enough trouble with Katie, who wasn't cooperating at all. She kept thrashing around while Megan towed her in. "Quit kicking!" Megan hissed in her ear.

"I'm trying to make it look real!" Katie yelled back.

Finally, they got the two victims to the side of the pool, and hoisted them up. Then they turned and faced the audience.

The families applauded, and the girls took a bow.

"Encore! Encore!" Someone yelled. One of Katie's brothers started booing, but Katie's father shut him up.

Erin ran up to Carolyn, got a hairbrush from her, and frantically started fixing her hair. Trina joined her mother, and Katie ran over to her family.

"Sarah, wait," Megan said as Sarah started

toward her father. "I want to show you this new stroke I learned."

"Right now?" Sarah asked.

"Yeah, watch me, okay?" Megan dove back into the pool. Underwater, she swam to the middle of the pool, and stayed at the bottom as long as she could. When she finally surfaced, she made loud gasping sounds. "Sarah, help me!" she screamed. "Help! Help!"

She knew she'd given a good performance from the look on Sarah's face. And Sarah reacted just the way Megan hoped she would.

She jumped into the water. With strong, sure strokes, she swam to Megan. Megan tried to make it easier by lying still, but it wasn't even necessary. Sarah's hold made it impossible for her to move. Stroking with one arm, she dragged Megan to the side of the pool.

Megan pulled herself out, and Sarah followed her. "Are you okay," Sarah asked anxiously. Then she turned a startled face and wide eyes to the audience, who had started applauding again. Her own father was standing up and yelling, "Bravo! Bravo!"

Her eyes got even wider when she saw Megan take another bow. "Megan! I thought you were really drowning!"

Megan grinned. "That's what you were supposed to think!"

Sarah's mouth fell open. "You tricked me!"

Megan nodded happily. "I knew you just needed a little push to get you going."

Meanwhile, Trina and Katie had run over to them. "You didn't tell us you were going to do that!" Katie accused Megan.

"I didn't know I was going to do it until today," Megan explained. She turned to Sarah. "You're not mad at me, are you?"

"I haven't decided yet," Sarah said. Then she looked back at the stands.

Nobody was laughing. Sarah's father joined them and grabbed his daughter in a big bear hug. "Sarah, you can swim! I'm really impressed!"

"Oh, I swim all the time," Sarah said carelessly. Then she winked at Megan. And Megan knew that this time she'd actually managed to pull off a fantasy scheme.

She wandered over to where her parents were standing with Carolyn.

"Excellent performance!" her father announced. "And that was a fine encore."

"Thanks," Megan said. "What's an encore?"

"That's when you repeat a performance," Carolyn told her. Megan felt very smug. She'd pulled it off! And nobody knew she'd tricked Sarah.

But then she realized Carolyn was eyeing her thoughtfully. "Megan, did you plan this? Was this another one of your fantasies at work?"

Megan opened her eyes wide. "Huh?"

115

Carolyn shook her head ruefully, but she was smiling. "Oh Megan, what *are* we going to do with you?"

Megan just continued to look innocent. Then she noticed something out of the corner of her eye.

Trina's mother and Sarah's father were talking together. And Megan remembered that Sarah's father was a widower, and Trina's mother was divorced.

An idea exploded in her head. What if they fell in love? It would be fantastic! Sarah and Trina would be sisters!

"Megan!"

She blinked, and saw that Carolyn was looking at her in alarm. "Megan, what are you thinking about?"

Megan grinned. "Just daydreaming. That's all."

Carolyn folded her arms. "Just remember your promise, okay? Those daydreams stay in your head!"

Megan nodded solemnly. "I remember." With firm resolve, she tried to push the fantasy out of her head. And she went back to join the others.

But as she walked across the pool landing, she passed Trina and her mother, Sarah and her father. They looked nice together, like a family.

And maybe, with just a little help . . .

116

If you enjoyed this
CAMP SUNNYSIDE FRIENDS
adventure...

Look for
TREEHOUSE TIMES

Coming In October 1989!

Four friends get together in a backyard
treehouse to start a neighborhood news-
paper, and the fun begins! They are hot
on the news trail and it leads right
smack into the middle of adventure
every time. Don't miss a single book!

Available from

AVON CAMELOT